"I'm not sure that's a good idea, Genevieve."

"It's not a good idea that I come with you?" He didn't need to answer. It'd been clear in his tone. "I brought you this case. Don't you think I should be the one to make the call whether or not I'm involved?"

"This killer challenged his victims to stop him. He's made it clear you're his next obsession, and I can't protect you if you're not trying to protect yourself."

"And I can't make sure he pays for what he's done if you lock me in my room," she countered. "Do you think because you kissed me I'm going to let you do this without me? He might already have his next victim."

"Do you want to end up like them?" The collapse of his defense took physical form as he stumbled back a step, and in that moment, she wasn't exactly sure which Easton she was talking to. The former fiancé, the soldier who'd survived Afghanistan or the Battle Mountain PD officer.

"I can't lose you again!"

DEAD GIVEAWAY

—

NICHOLE SEVERN

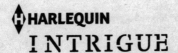

For Marla for equating my books to "Hallmark with guns."

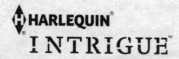

HARLEQUIN®
INTRIGUE™

ISBN-13: 978-1-335-48947-0

Dead Giveaway

Copyright © 2022 by Natascha Jaffa

Recycling programs for this product may not exist in your area.

This edition published by arrangement with Harlequin Books S.A.

For questions and comments about the quality of this book, please contact us at CustomerService@Harlequin.com.

Harlequin Enterprises ULC
22 Adelaide St. West, 41st Floor
Toronto, Ontario M5H 4E3, Canada
www.Harlequin.com

Printed in U.S.A.

Nichole Severn writes explosive romantic suspense with strong heroines, heroes who dare challenge them and a hell of a lot of guns. She resides with her very supportive and patient husband, as well as her demon spawn, in Utah. When she's not writing, she's constantly injuring herself running, rock climbing, practicing yoga and snowboarding. She loves hearing from readers through her website, www.nicholesevern.com, and on Facebook, @nicholesevern.

Books by Nichole Severn

Harlequin Intrigue

Defenders of Battle Mountain

Grave Danger
Dead Giveaway

A Marshal Law Novel

The Fugitive
The Witness
The Prosecutor
The Suspect

Blackhawk Security

Rules in Blackmail
Rules in Rescue
Rules in Deceit
Rules in Defiance
Caught in the Crossfire
The Line of Duty

Midnight Abduction
Profiling a Killer

Visit the Author Profile page at Harlequin.com.

CAST OF CHARACTERS

Easton Ford—Battle Mountain's only reserve officer refuses to let old feelings get in the way of protecting his hometown, but when bodies start piling up around his ex-fiancée, he can't ignore their past anymore. Or the demons he's kept buried.

Genevieve Alexander—She thought the nightmare was over. But prosecuting a copycat is just the beginning. There's only one man she trusts to protect her: the ex-fiancé she left at the altar. But Easton isn't the same man she remembers, and the secrets he's keeping from her might get them both killed.

The Contractor—This killer likes to put his work on display, and he's got his sights on Genevieve.

Weston Ford—Police chief of Battle Mountain and Easton's brother.

Battle Mountain—Rocky Mountains mining town consisting of 2,800 residents.

Chapter One

Her keys cut into the palm of her hand.

Genevieve Alexander couldn't move, couldn't think. She hadn't gotten more than two steps into the house before her instincts had warned her to run. The backs of her knees shook as she took in the blood. Shadows distorted the face of the victim, but she didn't need the lights on to identify the woman staring back at her. The killer's MO was already familiar, but crime scene photos were nothing compared to the real thing.

The Contractor.

It was impossible. The killer she'd prosecuted for stringing his victims from their own ceilings like marionettes had been sentenced to life behind bars without parole. This… This was something else. This was her home.

But the holes the medical examiner would find in each joint of the victim's body weren't the worst part.

Posed with the help of industrial-strength fishing line and steel eyelet screws, the woman stood there as though she'd simply been waiting for Genevieve to come home from work.

Because she had been. Waiting.

Reality pierced through paralyzing confusion and fear. Unpocketing her phone, she stumbled away from the scene in her once pristine living room. She couldn't contaminate the scene.

She collided with a wall of muscle.

Her scream cut short as a gloved hand clamped over her mouth.

"Hello, Genevieve." The unfamiliar voice grated against every cell in her body as he hauled her back into his chest. "Do you like my gift? I made her for you."

She struggled against the grip around her face and midsection. Head craned back, she couldn't see more than the blood spatter across her ceiling, and panic infused her nervous system. She clutched her phone, stretching her thumb across the screen to dial 9-1-1, but the man at her back was so much stronger, so much bigger. A hit of spiced cologne burned the back of her throat.

He pressed his mouth against her ear. "Drop the phone. I wouldn't want anyone disturbing us until I'm ready."

Genevieve shook her head. No. It was her only

lifeline. Her only guarantee she didn't end up like the victim on the other side of the room. Tears burned in her eyes. Pain lightninged through her lower back, and she arched against her attacker. Her protest died in his hand.

"You always try to control the situation on your terms. That's what makes you such a good district attorney, but the only way you're going to get through this tonight is if you do exactly as I say." A prick of pain centered over her throat. A blade? "Understand?"

She tapped her thumb against the screen, unsure if she'd hit the right buttons. She loosened her grip around the device. The hard *thunk* of metal meeting hardwood was as loud as the final nail in her own coffin. Had the call gone through? Her hair tugged at the base of her skull as she tried to lift her head, but he held her secure.

"Good. Now, I'm going to remove my hand from your mouth. If you scream, you die. If you attempt to escape or overpower me, you die," he said. "Any questions?"

Genevieve shook her head. She had to play along, had to do whatever it took to survive. Her exhales warmed the skin around her mouth as he peeled his gloved grip from her face. Closing her eyes, she recalled the layout of the house, where she'd stashed the gun she'd received as an engagement gift all those years ago. Her gaze settled on the brick fire-place a mere three feet from the victim, the one she'd taped her weapon inside. Had he searched the house? Had he already found it? Only one way to find out. "What do you want?"

"To give you one last chance to prove yourself." Her attacker smoothed her hair over her shoulder. Too close. Her gut revolted at his touch, but she'd have to buy her time before making her move. "Ms. Johnson here was nice enough to keep me company while I waited for you to come home. Unfortunately, she couldn't talk much after I drilled the first hole in her knee. I always pegged her for a better conversationalist, but now I know better."

Elisa Johnson? The contours of her assistant's features sharpened against the shadows threatening to consume her, and Genevieve's heart squeezed in her chest. Fire-red hair clung to the curves of an oval face and interrupted the flawless outline of full lips. Pale skin had lightened in the wash of moonlight, but it was her eyes that demanded attention. Impossibly green and empty. Her knees weakened, but the solid mass at her back refused to let her fall. She tried to process his last words, but escape had overridden any sense of logic. "I don't know what you're talking about. What do you mean you're giving me a chance to prove myself? I don't know you."

"But I know you, Genevieve. Did you think the

Contractor would be so easy to apprehend? That I'd let some random amateur with a grudge tarnish my name like that?" A growl vibrated through his chest and straight into her. "I've spent a year building my reputation, and one case with all the answers you're looking for comes along, and you just roll over. Is that what it's come to these days? You're supposed to make sense of the evidence. Not make it fit your personal agenda, Counselor."

Thousands of crime scene photos, half a dozen incident reports, countless witness interviews and investigation reports filed through her mind in less time than it took for her to take her next breath. "You're...you're lying. We have the right man. He confessed."

"Everyone wants to be known for something, don't they?" he asked. "Isn't that why you became district attorney? Isn't that why you bury yourself in your work during your sixteen-hour days, why you handle all of your cases personally and try to fill that missing piece you've been living with for so long?"

He'd studied her. Stalked her. Learned about her.

The blade dug into her skin as he maneuvered her back into the living room, but Genevieve wouldn't flinch. Wouldn't cry. She wouldn't give him the satisfaction. Her heels scraped against the hardwood floor. His grip slid to the nape of her neck, forcing her to confront the victim. Genevieve closed her eyes, but there was no erasing the images left behind.

"Look at her, Genevieve." He shook her hard enough to make her back teeth hit together. Leaning in, he leveled his gaze in her peripheral vision, but it was still too dark to make out anything significant. "Elisa Johnson is dead because you disappointed me. Out of everyone who worked that investigation, I expected you to see the lies, but maybe I've given you too much credit. Don't worry. I'm going to give you one more chance to become the opponent I deserve."

Once more chance? Genevieve forced herself to take a deep breath. Her attention cut to the fireplace. Her heart threatened to beat straight out of her chest. She had one shot to make it out of this alive. She wasn't going to fail. "You don't have to do this. You don't have to hurt anyone else."

"Sure, I do. Otherwise, what's the point?" he asked.

Sirens echoed through the large living room, growing closer. Red and blue patrol lights cut through her sheer curtains and sped around the room. Relief and panic combined in a twisted tornado of emotion. She couldn't let him get away. She couldn't let him do this to someone else.

"Seems our time together has come to an end, Genevieve, but I know we'll meet again." The grip at the back of her neck lightened, the pain in her back subsiding. "I promised to give you one more chance, and I'm a man of my word. Show me I didn't make a mistake when I chose you."

Genevieve ignored the bite of pain at her throat as she lunged for the fireplace. The corner of the brick crushed the air from her lungs, but she shot her hand up into the chimney and ripped the gun she'd duct-taped there free. Spinning to confront the killer, she took aim at an empty room. Her breath sawed in and out of her chest. Sweat built in her hairline as shouts penetrated the bubble of fear in her chest. She heard the front door slam against the wall behind it, and in a split second, flashlight beams centered on her. Then the body.

"Drop the weapon! Interlace your hands behind your head!" An officer closed in on her, then slowed. Disbelief hitched his voice an octave higher. "Ms. Alexander, put the gun on the floor, turn around and interlace your hands behind your head. Now."

"He was here." Her fingers shook as the past few minutes replayed in her head. She tried to keep her voice even despite the storm churning inside. He'd said he'd chosen her, that he wanted her to prove herself. What did that mean? What did Elise Johnson have to do with any of it? She released her grip on the weapon, catching the trigger cage around her index finger and slowly placed her gun on the floor. "He was here."

But he'd be long gone by now. Most likely through

the trees surrounding the back half of her property, and he'd left Elise behind to remind her of her failure to bring him down. They hadn't been able to connect the Contractor's victims, but he'd chosen her assistant for a reason.

Because of her.

An officer collected her weapon from the floor while another maneuvered behind her. Wrenching her arms at her lower back, he secured both wrists into cuffs. The ratcheting of metal seemed louder in that moment. Two others arced their flashlights over the victim's face, her hands, clothing and legs. They took in the bloody screws installed at each of the body's joints. The drill holes would measure out to be caused by a 5/16 drill bit once the medical examiner had a chance to do the autopsy. Just like the others.

Only that wasn't true. Air caught in her throat. She hadn't seen it before now, she'd been too caught up in the investigation at the time. The last victim, the one they'd connected back to the man they believed to be the Contractor. Corey Singleton. He'd used a 3/8 drill bit.

He hadn't been the Contractor at all.

He'd been the copycat.

"What the hell is that?" one of the uniforms asked.

Her attention slid to the woman at her side, strung up for all to see. The answer to his question settled at the front of her mind. Her voice deadpanned as she realized the outfit she'd carefully chosen this morning before heading into the office had been stained with the victim's blood. She rose to her feet at the officer's cue, the world clearer than it'd ever been before. Her mouth dried as she considered the implications of what'd just happened. "My punishment."

"ACCORDING TO ALAMOSA POLICE, a suspect in the death of Elisa Johnson's horrific murder has been arrested and is in custody for questioning. District Attorney Genevieve Alexander was found at her home, holding a gun at police as they responded to the 9-1-1 call from Alexander's cell phone. Upon arrival, police discovered the mutilated body of Johnson and blood matching the victim's DNA on the DA's clothing."

Genevieve.

Easton Ford twisted toward the television. He lunged for the remote, knocking it to the floor in the too-small cabin, and hit the volume button. The news anchor went on to warn viewers and small children before plastering photos from the crime scene across the screen. Hell. The positioning of the body, the amount of blood left behind… He'd seen the worst in people stationed overseas—survived the worst—but this was different. This was sociopathic. B-roll video of Alamosa PD's main suspect answering questions outside the courthouse replaced the horrific images of the scene.

A surge of familiarity knotted in his gut. Wavy dark brown hair, wide almond-shaped eyes and flawless skin triggered his protective instincts as he watched Genevieve in her element in front of the camera. The deep red blouse and black skirt clung to her lean frame like a second skin, but it was the honesty and brightness in her eyes that compelled him to take a step forward. The numbers in the corner of the screen dated the video a couple months old, but, even after all this time, she hadn't changed much at all. How long had it been? Fifteen years? More? He'd been a silly kid in love with his high school sweetheart, ready to take on the world for her.

Before the world had taught him happily-ever-afters didn't exist.

Not for him.

Three knocks punctured through the focused haze he had on the TV, and he hit the power button. It'd been months since he'd picked up a weapon, but his instincts automatically had him wanting to reach for the safe under his bed. He was being paranoid. The only people who dared to knock on his door out here in the middle of nowhere were his mother and the pain-in-the-ass police chief of Battle Mountain. His brother.

A growl of irritation built in his chest. As the most recent volunteer reserve officer for Battle Mountain PD, he'd taken the brunt of shifts these past few months since Weston had gone and gotten himself a fiancée, but today was his day off. Easton tossed the remote onto the couch. Three steps. That was all it took to cross his small satellite cabin on his family's property.

Whispering Pines Ranch had become more of a retreat to tourists and strangers than a safe haven recently, but his father's death two months ago had made an increase in reservations necessary to keep the ranch running. His mother was doing the best she could, but his intention to disappear—to detach—from the world and everybody in it was getting harder to accomplish every time some tourist needed directions.

He ripped the door back on its hinges, prepared to reestablish the rules of the ranch.

And froze.

"Hi." One word. That was it. She stood there as though he hadn't seen police escort her from her home in Alamosa in cuffs or the blood staining her clothing on the news mere minutes ago. As though she hadn't left him at the altar on their wedding day. As though she hadn't gutted his heart before an IED had tried to finish the job in Afghanistan. Genevieve Alexander, in the flesh. Her hair whipped into her face as spring struggled to hang on a little bit longer. "I heard you were back in the States."

Easton crossed his arms over his chest and leaned against the door frame. Scanning the property, he pegged what he assumed was her vehicle parked along the dirt driveway. Damn. He hadn't even heard her coming. Too distracted by the news that she'd been found in the middle of one of the most gruesome crime scenes in history. "I heard you were arrested for your assistant's murder."

"That's why I'm here." She swiped her hair away from her face, exposing the delicate pattern of bruises across the front of her throat. "I didn't kill Elisa. I found her dead, strung up like a puppet, when I got home from work. The man who killed her. He was waiting for me in the house."

He pushed off from the door frame, gaze locked on the outline of a thumb print along the side of her neck. An uncontrollable heat exploded through him as Easton closed the distance between them. He pushed her hair out of the way to get a better look. "Who?"

"I don't know. I was in the middle of calling 9-1-1 when he attacked me. I wasn't sure the call had gone through until the police were breaking down my front door." Genevieve seemed to curl in on herself, deep green eyes distant as she lowered her attention to his boots. "Alamosa PD didn't have any other choice but to take me into custody when they responded to the call. They found me at the scene, covered in the Elisa's blood—"

"With a gun in your hand," he said.

She nodded. "I kept it taped to the inside of my

chimney for protection. The work I do and the people I prosecute… I make enemies. I didn't want to be unprepared, but I never expected this. I told the police everything he said to me. They're still trying to corroborate I'd just left the courthouse fifteen minutes prior to the call, but they don't have any evidence to file charges. So I was released a few hours ago."

"And you came here." Genevieve didn't have the inclination or the strength to hang a woman from the ceiling, and the evidence of bruising around the back of her neck said she was telling the truth. Someone had attacked her.

"I didn't know where else to go. I need your help, Easton." She set her chin. "You have every right to hate me after what I did, but whoever killed Elisa Johnson is going to kill again. He's doing this because of me, and you're the only one I can trust to handle yourself while I investigate."

"You want to take on a killer without the support of the police." Battle-ready tension hardened the muscles down his spine. Easton pulled his shoulders back, and suddenly, she seemed so much smaller than a minute ago. "What do you mean he's doing this because of you?"

"That's why he killed Elisa. That's why he was waiting for me in my house." Her voice shook. Unlike anything he'd heard before. "Have you heard of the Contractor?"

His instincts kicked into overdrive, and everything inside of him went cold. Easton stepped back. The victim in Genevieve's home. He'd seen that kind of depravity before. "Serial killer. Strung his victims up from the ceiling using fishing line and steel eyelets. You think he has something to do with this?"

"I think he *is* this." Another tendril of breeze filtered through her hair and released the hint of her perfume as she countered his escape. "The man who killed my assistant isn't the same man I prosecuted for the deaths of those four women. He's...disappointed in me for falling for a copycat, disappointed that I took his reputation from him."

"And you believed him?" he asked.

"I prosecuted Corey Singleton on four counts of first-degree murder. The investigating detectives recovered trace DNA from the last scene that pointed them to Singleton. He had a history of violence, a connection with the last victim and was in possession of the drill bit used to burrow holes into the victim's joints. Forensics matched the blood on the drill to her almost immediately." Color drained from her face. "I had everything I needed to prosecute him for the first three deaths through evidence from that scene alone, but there was something different about the last victim compared to the other three. I didn't make the connection until it was too late."

Pressure built behind his sternum the longer

Easton let her work her way back into his life. "What connection?"

"Corey Singleton used a 3/18 drill bit to kill his last victim, but the first three? They were murdered using a 5/16th," she said. "I know it doesn't sound like much, but if the man who killed Elisa was lying, why the change in tools? Serial killers have a compulsion to carry out their kills systematically. There's a ritual behind this, an origin story. Something police were never able to pinpoint with Singleton."

"There are any number of reasons for the change. He could've broken the original drill bit, lost it. Maybe he made the change to do exactly what you're doing right now. Throw doubt on the investigation and his guilt. It's obvious Singleton didn't kill your assistant as he's serving the rest of his life behind bars, but the man waiting for you in your home could easily be the copycat. Why take him at his word?" Awareness charged through his veins as her perfume infiltrated his personal space. What the hell was he doing here? What was it about Genevieve that pulled him in to the point he could momentarily forget what she'd done?

"Because I was there," she said. "I heard the truth in his voice."

"You and I both know that wouldn't hold up in court, Counselor." No. He couldn't put himself through this again. Not after he'd just started to get his balance under the crushing weight of grief. For his father two months ago. For his unit he hadn't been able to save last year. He'd done his part in bringing down a killer determined to rip his family apart. He wouldn't put them through that again. He wouldn't lose anyone else.

Easton forced himself to detach, to take a step back. He set his hand on the doorknob, and that mesmerizing gaze honed on the movement. "You've got an entire police force capable of uncovering the truth and protecting you, Genevieve. I'm not one of them."

He moved to close the door.

She slammed her hand against it. Fire simmered in her gaze, and a responding heat flared under his rib cage. "I read the papers, Easton. I know you had a hand in apprehending that man who killed those three victims here in Battle Mountain, including your father. He targeted your future sister-in-law. Someone you didn't even know." Genevieve let her fingers slip down the weathered wood of the cabin's front door and straightened. "Please. Whoever's doing this… He's not going to stop. He wants to prove he's the real Contractor. He believes I'm a key player in his game, and I'm scared. I can't do this without you."

The old brass doorknob protested under his grip. "Then I suggest you start running."

He closed the door behind him.

Chapter Two

She was on her own.

Genevieve shoved the two-decades-old key into the scratched faceplate and pushed inside. A wall of odor burned down her throat as she closed the door behind her. Battle Mountain, Colorado had once been the state's most industrious mining town. But when the mines went out of business and residents had to leave their birthplace for stable employment and income, the town had taken a major hit. Money had dried up, tourism had yet to recover, and places like Cindy's Motel had started showing their age.

The single-level structure stretched between the dilapidated parking lot and overgrown ring of trees. Light blue paint peeled away from the popcorn ceiling and flaked down into the corners of the room. Worn brown carpet came up at the edges and matted in the center of the room. She tossed her keys on the dresser near the door. The beds had been professionally made up, but there wasn't an inch of her body that wanted any contact with those sheets. Sunlight filtered through the dirty window at the back of the room and from a smaller window in the bathroom on the other side of the dresser.

It wasn't much. It wasn't anything, but the thought of going back to Alamosa, of stepping inside that house, nauseated her iron stomach. The life she'd built since leaving Battle Mountain on her wedding day was over. There was no going back, even if Alamosa PD released the scene. Right now, Cindy's was all she had.

Genevieve unshouldered her bag onto the bed. The white noise of cars traveling down Main reached her ears, but where she'd once found comfort in being surrounded by people she'd known all her life, fear tunneled deeper. Someone had broken into her home three nights ago, had killed her assistant and left her for Genevieve to find. He'd put his hand over her mouth and bruised the back of her neck. Her fingers automatically traced the pucker of scabs along her throat. The blade hadn't gone deep, but it would leave a scar. Something for her to carry the rest of her life.

She closed the blackout curtains over the window, encasing herself in darkness. Too exposed. She fumbled for the lamp on the nightstand between the beds. Light clawed up the walls and across the floor as she sat on the edge of the mattress. Her hair slid in front of her shoulder as she reached for her bag. Tugging the folder of files she'd printed from the backup on her laptop before Alamosa PD had taken it into evidence, she bit back the urge to break. Crime scene photos, investigation reports, witness statements— it was all there.

I promised to give you one more chance, and I'm a man of my word. Prove I didn't make a mistake when I chose you.

Genevieve shoved the folder back into her bag. Chose her for what? As another victim? If that'd been the case, he would've killed her then. Or maybe he'd run out of time. She tensed against the shiver cascading down her spine and forced herself to her feet. She was a district attorney, damn it. He didn't get to do this to her. He didn't get to haunt her for the rest of her life. She'd prosecuted the worst criminals in the state for more than five years. He should be the one to fear her. A humorless laugh escaped her lips as she confronted the mirror over the dresser. "What are you doing here?"

She'd known Easton wouldn't be happy to see her, but the moment Alamosa PD had finished interrogating her, he'd been the one to cross her mind. Not her staff. Not her friends. Not her parents or brother. Easton. She gripped the edge of the dresser, the ache in her fingers anchoring her to the moment. He'd been exactly as she remembered. Defensive. Evasive. Cautious. All the things that'd made him a survivor of war.

Once upon a time, they'd been dumb and in love. They'd had an entire future in front of them and not a single care in the world. A smile tugged at the corner of her mouth. Only it didn't last long, and it'd all come crashing down around her.

She'd felt the cracks starting between them long before he'd slipped that engagement ring on her finger, but Easton had been her first. Her first love. Her first kiss. Her first everything. She hadn't known anything about the world then or her place in it, not even what she wanted to do with her life. He was handsome, loyal and everything she'd been told she wanted in a husband. He'd loved his family and put everyone else's needs, including hers, before his own as his father had taught him. Then she'd gotten into that beautiful lacy dress the morning of their wedding. She'd always loved beautiful things, had a compulsion to surround herself with beauty as much as possible, but the only thing looking back at her while she stood in front of that mirror had been a stranger. A hollow capsule of flesh and bone she hadn't recognized for years.

So she'd run. She'd left the dress behind, the ring, left Battle Mountain and him. She'd worked two part-time jobs in a town less than three hours away to pay for law school and strived to become her own woman. Not Easton Ford's girlfriend, his fiancée or his wife. She'd heard through the small-town grape-

vine he'd joined the army two weeks after their wedding day, that he'd served his country all this time
until his unit had been ambushed last year. She'd
grieved. She'd blamed herself for driving him to escape, and the months had slipped by. Until she'd
learned he'd survived.

What was she supposed to do now? The police
suspected her of having something to do with Elisa's
murder, even though she'd been the one to call the
police, and there was no evidence of blood on the
tools her father had given her when she'd bought the
house. They wouldn't let her near the investigation,
and the law prohibited her from prosecuting a case
where she was involved. Not only that but the one
man she believed she could rely on had closed the
door in her face. She was alone.

Genevieve raised her gaze to the mirror. She
wasn't a detective. She wasn't an investigator. A single moment of terror had ripped the life she'd built
from her hands. She'd relied on her work to get her
through the worst lows she'd survived. Now all she
had was a case file and memories of that night. It
would have to be enough. Because the thought of
letting another woman die as Elisa Johnson had…

She slid the folder from her bag a second time and
forced herself to open it. Spreading the photos across
the bed, she took them all in at once. The similari-
ties in the manner of death, the differences in each

victim's appearance, the investigative style of the detectives assigned to each case. She tried to breathe through the sob lodged in her throat as she added her assistant's file to the mass of reports.

The police had already started their investigation. She would finish it.

Fishing the roll of Scotch tape from her bag, she secured the first victim's photo to the right side of the mirror, followed by photos of the scene. Genevieve stepped back. She'd been through these files hundreds of times to prove the evidence implicated Corey Singleton in the four murders. Now she'd prove someone else had killed the first three victims.

Maria Gutierrez. Twenty-eight, single, lived alone with no connections to any of the other victims. Soft black hair framed a heart-shaped face and highlighted the richness of the victim's skin. She'd been beautiful with a wide smile in the photographs her parents had given to police. Genevieve remembered them from Singleton's trial, remembered their tears and heartfelt appreciation for putting the animal who'd killed their daughter behind bars. Only now, she wasn't so sure she had. She couldn't imagine what they—what the other families—were feeling with the possibility she'd been wrong. They'd gotten their closure. But it seemed someone was determined to make them relive that loss all over again. She couldn't think about that. Maria had been the first victim. She'd just graduated with her master's in psychology. She'd been preparing to apply to the FBI as one of their criminal investigators with her eye on joining the Behavioral Analysis Unit.

Genevieve crossed her arms over her chest to control the tremors in her hands. She stepped closer to the dresser, studying every pixel of the crime scene photos as though it were the first time. There had to be something here. Serial killers like the one who'd broken into her home didn't wake up and start killing one morning. Something had set him off. Something had attracted him to Maria Gutierrez and the next three victims. "Why was she so special to you?"

She caught sight of Maria Gutierrez's front door. The LED light on the alarm panel was green. No sign of forced entry. Just as there'd been no sign of a break-in at her own home. Police posited Maria had disarmed the panel to answer the door. From there, the killer had forced his way inside. She pulled the photo free of the vanity mirror. No. That didn't make sense. Maria had been fit, training every day to pass the Bureau's physical exam. She kept herself in shape because she knew what it would take to become an agent. She would've fought back, but there hadn't been DNA under her fingernails or defensive wounds. "You let him into the house. You knew him."

Why hadn't she seen it before? Why hadn't police?

Genevieve turned back to the investigation file. Detectives would've interviewed the victim's friends, her family, coworkers—everyone in her life—to get a sense of her routine and behavior leading up to her death to narrow down their suspect pool. She shuffled through the case file, speed-reading through handwritten notes and typed reports. Witness statements didn't reveal any unusual activity in the days leading up to Maria Gutierrez's death, but the victim's phone records told a different story.

There.

A call from Maria's cell phone to 9-1-1 two weeks before she'd been discovered strung up by fishing line had been singled out among hundreds of others between the victim and her friends and family. Police had foolishly dismissed it as part of the investigation because of the timeline, but Genevieve's instincts screamed there was a connection. The call hadn't lasted more than thirty seconds, barely enough time to report a crime to the dispatcher, but it was something. She raised her gaze to the smiling photo of the Contractor's first victim taped to the mirror. "What scared you enough to call the police, Maria? What did you see?"

GENEVIEVE WASN'T GOING to run.

She hadn't become district attorney by shying away from a challenge. Only this challenge was sure to get her killed, and hell, if he wouldn't be the one responsible for it. She might've ripped out his heart the day of their wedding, but his father had taught him better than to turn his back on someone in need.

Damn the old man's sense of honor.

Easton forced one foot in front of the other across the parking lot, the to-go bag in his hand. Word at Greta's on Main, the only diner in town, put Genevieve over at Cindy's Motel down the block. The place wasn't much. Multiple rooms lined up one after the other, and there at the end was the same junker car that'd been parked in his driveway this morning. He'd already run the plates. Question was, had Genevieve stolen the vehicle or borrowed it from the owner legally? He bet the latter, considering she wouldn't have wanted to draw extra attention. No more than being Alamosa PD's main person of interest in a homicide investigation.

He jogged across Main and walked straight up to the door. He raised his fist to knock, but it swung inward before he had the chance. A small gasp reached his ears as Genevieve stumbled back. His awareness honed in on the small differences between the woman he'd watched on TV to the one recoiling in front of him. The lack of makeup, the shadows under her eyes, the slight feralness of her hair. Red ringed her eyes as though she hadn't slept in days. Not to mention the fact that she wore an oversized sweater and jeans instead of one of those power suits she'd taken on as armor over the course of her career. It'd only been three days since the attack, but it was obvious Genevieve Alexander wasn't the same. He offered her the bag. "Figured you probably hadn't eaten. I brought your favorite. Waffles from Greta's. Consider it a peace offering."

"How did you know I was here?" She took the bag and peered inside, careful not to touch him. Her expression contorted into confusion. "And where is my bacon?"

"I think you know the answer to both of those questions." He wiped at his mouth to ensure he hadn't left any bacon crumbs or grease behind.

"You never could help yourself, even after I stabbed your hand with my fork at your family's breakfast one Sunday." The momentary crack in expression revealed the same deadpanned humor he'd come to love about her all those years ago. It electrified his nerves but disappeared before he had a chance to lose himself into her gravitational pull. Genevieve stared down at the white plastic bag. "I know you, Easton. You didn't come all the way down the mountain to bring me waffles, and given what you said to me this morning, I know you haven't suddenly had a change of heart. So what do you want from me?"

The warmth between them vanished as quickly

as her smile, and the hollowness he'd carried since discovering her engagement ring in the bride's suite of the church flared. "You were right before. My brother and his fiancée were targeted by a serial offender two months ago, and I was part of the investigation. While I don't have as much experience on the force as the Alamosa PD, I have a key set of skills they don't. Mostly intelligence gathering. So after you left—"

"You mean after you told me to start running and shut the door in my face," she said.

Heat scorched down his spine as defiance claimed her expression. Despite distance and time, some things hadn't changed. But he had. "After your visit this morning, I took a look at Alamosa PD's reports on the Contractor killings in National Criminal Information database and requested the original case files, but they only sent two. Seems the FBI took over after a second victim turned up, and seeing as how you were the prosecuting attorney, I assume you have access to the complete investigation file."

"Right." She stood a bit straighter, her attention drifting somewhere off to her right toward Main Street. "And if I said I have the files? What then? You made it pretty clear you didn't want anything to do with me or this investigation this morning. What changed?"

He set his top teeth over his bottom and tapped

them together at the sure horror of Battle Mountain's dentist, Dr. Corsey. Memories of loss, of suffocating, of screams and fire fought to escape the box he'd buried them inside. A low ringing started in his ears, and Easton closed his eyes to get ahead of the flashback. His heart rocketed higher, pounding behind his ears. He just had to ride it out and hope there was a small part left of himself when it ended.

"Easton?" Her voice penetrated through the ringing. Soft skin smoothed over the back of his hand, and in an instant, he was anchored in the moment. "Easton."

The ringing stopped. The panic dissipated, and he opened his eyes. She centered herself in his vision. He studied her hands wrapped around his and pulled back. Damn it. He'd had it under control. He'd managed for months, even after being buried alive in a freezer with his brother the night his father had been killed. But within hours of her coming back to town, his brain felt as though it'd been put in a blender on high power. He forced his breathing to slow, forced himself to stay in the moment.

"Are you okay?" Concern etched deep into her expression.

"I'm… I'm fine." He swiped damp palms down his jeans. Distraction. The case. "If you give me a chance to review the case file, I might be able to pull something on your killer. Something Alamosa PD might've missed."

Hesitation slowed her step back into the motel room, but Genevieve nodded. "Yeah, okay." She left the door open for him, and Easton stepped inside. She motioned to the vanity mirror. "This is everything I was able to download before the captain banned me from investigating the last victim's death and took my laptop as possible evidence. Five total, but the fourth—Kayleigh Winters—I'm positive was killed by Corey Singleton, the man I prosecuted, and not the Contractor."

Crime scene photos and investigation reports had been taped over every reachable inch of the main wall in the room. Five distinct victims complete with hot-pink sticky notes in Genevieve's handwriting, but the fourth—Kayleigh Winters—had been set apart from the others. Hell. She'd gone and made herself her own murder board. Then again, Genevieve always had been creative. "You've been busy."

"Yeah, well, when a serial killer breaks into your home to tell you he's the real killer, you need to see the whole story. Not individual pieces." She set the bag with the to-go container of waffles on the farthest bed from the door. Neither of the beds had been disturbed other than to act as a table for the papers she hadn't gotten around to hanging on the murder wall, but from what he'd been able to get out of

Greta at the diner, Genevieve had gotten into town last night. She obviously hadn't slept, or if she had, she'd taken the floor. No evidence of food containers other than the one he'd brought either. The district attorney had trained herself to put on a strong face, but the cracks had already started to show. If she kept this up, she wouldn't last the night.

Easton stepped into the web of photos and sticky notes and reports. Most of Genevieve's work seemed to center around one victim in particular. Phone records indicated the victim had made a call to 9-1-1 two weeks before her death. "What's so special about this call to police?"

"Maria Gutierrez was the first victim killed by the Contractor. This started with her." Genevieve closed the distance between them. "Serial killers rarely kill randomly. At least, the pattern isn't random to them. For the majority of the homicide cases I've prosecuted, the first victim ends up being someone the killer knew. I've gone over all of her friends' and family's statements. No one sticks out yet, but I thought if I figured out what made her so special to him, why he chose her—"

"You could determine a connection to the rest of his victims." It was the smart move and made the most sense. Something had to have triggered the killer. The answer could be in Maria Gutierrez's file.

"Yes." Genevieve folded her arms across her

chest. "Maria graduated with a master's in psychology. She was getting ready to apply to the Bureau with hopes of joining one of the BAU teams after doing her time in Criminal Investigation. I'm still in the process of trying to get a hold of the 9-1-1 recording. She might've seen something. Something that scared her enough to call police."

"You think she recognized our killer for what he was." And tried to stop him.

"It's possible. She was training herself to see the signs. I won't know for sure until I can review the recording, but I can't find any other instances in her life where she'd need to call 9-1-1," she said. "No one in her family had been hurt, there were no reports of accidents or break-ins in the area around her home. According to the GPS data from her phone, the call originated from her house, near midnight."

"Thirty seconds. That's not much time to explain you suspect someone in your life is a serial killer." Easton unpocketed his phone and speed-dialed Battle Mountain's police chief. His brother and boss. "I'll see what I can do about the recording. After that, we'll know if your theory is right."

The line rang.

Genevieve set both hands on her hips and stared up at the wall. "Thank you."

Two sharp knocks twisted Easton toward the still open door. A courier stepped into the room carrying a small cardboard box, a familiar insignia on his chest. "Hey, I've got a delivery for Genevieve Alexander."

"I...didn't order anything." Wide eyes met Easton's as the color washed from her face and neck. "No one knows I'm here."

Easton ended the call and reached for the box. "I'll take it."

"Have a nice day." The courier jogged back to his truck.

Turning the package over in his hand, he studied the label. Genevieve's name had been handwritten across the box with the motel's address and room number printed clearly below it in thick black marker. Easton slid his phone back into his pocket and pulled his tactical folding knife from the other. He cut through the tape and pried open the lid as Genevieve took position off to his right.

Packing material exposed the single item at the bottom of the box. Nausea churned in his gut as he set the box on the dresser. "I need to call this in."

Chapter Three

He'd found her.

She wasn't sure how, but there was no denying the box that'd been delivered had been meant for her. Genevieve pressed the crown of her head into the aged brick outside her room. Nothing helped. She could still see the blood, the outline of flesh and cartilage.

Weston Ford, Battle Mountain's police chief, had already swept her motel room and bagged the evidence. The coroner, Dr. Chloe Miles, would be able to tell them how long ago the ear had been cut from its owner once she could do a thorough examination. Maybe even whether or not the victim was male or female, possibly get an ID through DNA.

It didn't make sense. The Contractor had never dismembered victims before. Why would he start now? Why send the mutilated ear to her? Genevieve pressed her fingernails into her palms. It wasn't supposed to be like this. She wasn't supposed to be here.

"Do you have any idea of how he knew you were here?" Easton stepped into her peripheral vision. A day's worth of beard growth shadowed the sharp angles of his jaw. Two distinct lines deepened between his eyebrows as he closed one eye against the afternoon sun to look at her. Penetrating deep blue eyes settled on her, and a slow burn climbed up her spine. He hadn't changed much over the years. He'd always been handsome with a combination of his father's good looks and his mother's eyes, but there was something different about him, something weathered. Tested, to the point she couldn't look away.

"No." She shook her head to break the all too familiar spell he cast onto the people around him, the one that drew her into his eyes and urged her to drown in the depths. "I withdrew cash from an ATM in Alamosa before I got out of town and left my credit cards behind. I paid for the room in cash and purchased a phone that couldn't be linked to me. I even surrendered my laptop to the police so it couldn't connect to any networks without my knowing. He shouldn't have been able to find me."

"And your car?" He pulled a small notebook from his back pocket and scribbled unrecognizable notes into it. The seam of his flannel shirt protested against a breeze funneling down the canyon carved into the San Juan mountains.

"I borrowed it from a family member of another

case. I told her I needed it for a few days but didn't say where I was going. She said I could use it as long as I needed." Her voice leveled out of habit, masking the tornado of fear and anger spiraling out of control. "Mine is still parked in my garage."

"Then he followed you." Easton stabbed the pen into his notebook then pocketed both. "Weston and Chloe are still trying to determine where the box came from and who the ear belongs to. We've got DNA and tissue samples, but Battle Mountain doesn't have a forensics lab. It'll be a few days before Unified Forensics in Denver is able to determine any results. I put a call into the delivery company and got a hold of the driver. The warehouse had already loaded his truck by the time he got to work this morning. The box had all the required labels, but the company told Weston the package doesn't actually exist."

"You're saying the killer could've put it on the truck because it looks like all the others." It made sense, but having the answer didn't settle the agonizing buzz of anxiety under her skin. She bit into her thumbnail, an old habit she hadn't been able to kick. She studied the cars in the parking lot, memorizing every license plate, every scratch and dent and possible location the killer could've hidden. Had he been right outside her door this entire time? "Which makes it impossible to trace. What about the

driver? Have you talked to the warehouse employees
or pulled the security footage from the warehouse?"

Because there had to be something. A killer didn't
just walk into people's lives and right back out without leaving a trace.

"We ran a background check on the driver and
corroborated his alibi. He was at home helping his
wife and their colicky son when the truck was being
loaded. As for the security footage, we're working
on it. Unfortunately, Battle Mountain PD is a little
short-staffed. You're looking at one of two officers,
and the other one isn't the least bit happy I called,"
he said. "To be fair, Weston's never happy if he has
to leave his cabin these days, but that's not the point.
Until we can figure out who the hell is behind this,
it's not safe for you here alone."

A humorless laugh escaped up her throat, and
she dropped her hand to her side as she faced him.
"Where am I supposed to go, Easton? I did everything I was supposed to to make sure no one could
track me, but it wasn't enough. It doesn't matter
where I go. He's designed some kind of test I don't
know the answers to, and he's not going to stop leaving bodies behind."

"Then you're coming back to the ranch with me,"
he said.

The skin along her scalp constricted. No. She
nearly flinched against his suggestion. No. "You

can't be serious. A killer has marked me as a potential victim, and you want to bring me home with you. Where your family lives, where innocent civilians will be vacationing. You don't want me on your land, Easton."

"Not permanently, no, but it's the only choice you've got." He stepped into her, every inch the soldier she'd imagined these past few years. Committed. Reliable. Defiant. "We have six satellite cabins. Weston and Chloe are in one, I'm in another. Our last tourist left this morning. Mom is in the main house. You'll have your own space, and there's no chance whoever is doing this will find you there. I might not carry a firearm anymore, but the rest of my family does. We know the land. We know the threat. You'll be safe to investigate this case without the weight of being a psychopath's target under our watch. Isn't that the goal?"

She didn't know what to say to that. The logic of it made sense, but her heart warned her the minute she stepped foot on that ranch, surrounded by his family, unable to escape the pull he had on her— she'd be right back where she started. "Why are you doing this?"

"You're the one who asked for my help this morning, Genevieve," he said. "If it makes it any easier, I could always put you in cuffs. Just got myself a new pair a few weeks ago. Haven't had the chance to test them out." His eyes brightened at his own threat. "Besides, you and I both know Alamosa PD told you not to leave town while they conducted their investigation into your assistant's murder. You might be a district attorney, but that doesn't put you above the law. Having two BMPD officers vouch for your whereabouts if they come calling isn't a bad idea."

Damn his logic. Warmth flared up her neck and into her face. He was right. The police still considered her a person of interest, but she wasn't willing to wait for Elisa Johnson's killer to ambush her a second time. "Fine."

"Good." He headed for the familiar turquoise 1959 Chevy Fleetwood pickup with its bulbous headlights and smooth curves. The paint job was new. At least within the past few years. He'd always had a soft spot for the hunk of junk considering how uncomfortable she remembered the seats were. Calling over his shoulder, he hit her with a half smile that knocked the wind straight out of her. "Grab what you need but be advised. Your little art project probably won't fit in the cabin."

Dr. Chloe Miles, soon to be Ford, stepped from the motel room with the cardboard box in one bag and the ear in another. The coroner's long dark hair had been pulled back, exaggerating her beautiful Latina heritage and deep-set eyes. Pristine slacks and a button-down shirt clung to the doctor's lean frame.

"Not a lot of people can find a body part in their mail and hold it together like you have."

"As much as I wish it wasn't true, I've seen my share. I know how these things go." She stretched out her hand. "Genevieve Alexander."

Understanding widened the coroner's eyes for a fraction of a second before Dr. Miles tried to hide her surprise. Too late. The good doctor shook her hand. "I heard about what happened to your assistant in Alamosa. I'm sorry for your loss."

"Thank you." She didn't know what else to say. For as many hours and she and Elisa had spent together going over her court schedule and requesting files to review, Genevieve hadn't known her assistant well. They weren't friends. They barely spoke of anything more than the job, but that small connection had been enough for Elisa to become a target. Genevieve took a single step forward, her voice shakier than she meant. "Dr. Miles, two months ago you were almost killed by a man who buried his victims alive in refrigerators. I've reviewed the police reports. I've read your statement, but what I can't figure out is how you did it."

Apprehension filtered across the coroner's expression, and Chloe hugged the evidence closer to her chest. "How I did what?"

"Survive." She needed to know, needed to see the

mind game she'd been recruited to participate in had another outcome other than her death.

Dr. Miles nodded, understanding. "Sometimes I'm not so sure I did. Survive. I still have nightmares. I still wake up feeling as though I'm locked in that container, and I'm running out of air." Police Chief Weston Ford maneuvered around them before heading for Easton on the other side of the parking lot, and the coroner's gaze followed him the entire way. A small tug of the muscles at the corner of her mouth betrayed her inner thoughts, and a ping of envy slithered through Genevieve. "Having Weston there to remind me that the man who hurt us and Easton is behind bars helps, but it doesn't make the nightmares any less real."

Easton?

"What do you do then?" A knot of tension solidified in her gut.

"I force myself to remember. What he looked like, how his voice sounded, the smell of his cologne. I put myself back in that refrigerator, and I make myself face the pain all over again to retrain my body not to react. Sometimes it helps. Sometimes it doesn't. Either way, having someone you can trust to be there with you is key." Dr. Miles's smile slipped away as she raised molten-brown eyes to Genevieve. "The thing about fear, Ms. Alexander, is that you have the power to control it. If you don't, you can guarantee it will control you."

THE TRUCK BOUNCED beneath them as Easton accelerated back toward Whispering Pines. His seat protested with each jerk of the shocks, the passenger side window didn't roll all the way up anymore and there was a smell he hadn't quite been able to locate yet. But damn if Genevieve shoving her hair away from her face from the passenger seat didn't throw him back into the past. When life had been simpler and neither of them had known what was coming. "Weston is interviewing the warehouse workers from the shipping company. He should be able to get access to their security footage, too. If we're lucky, we'll know exactly who put that package on the truck."

"Everything about four of the five murders has been planned down to the last detail. No forensics at the scenes. No witness statements." Genevieve kept her gaze out the passenger side window. "Do you really think he's going to slip this late in the game and risk being caught on camera?"

No. He didn't, but it was a lead they didn't have before.

Main Street shops constructed in various shades of red brick and flowering clusters of previously winter-stripped trees thinned as they left Battle Mountain town limits. Monstrous peaks demanded attention as they headed west, only a few strips of snow still clinging to the mountains.

"Thank you," she said. "For helping me. I'm sure I'm the last person you wanted to show up on your doorstep this morning."

"To be fair, I don't want anyone showing up on my doorstep." He turned onto an unpaved road a mile or so outside of town and maneuvered through a combination of mountainous ridges and family-owned ranches. Muscle memory kicked into gear as he took in the gut-wrenching openness of Mother Nature stretched out in front of them. He wasn't exactly sure how long it'd been since Genevieve had been out this way, whether or not she'd visited Battle Mountain since running all those years ago. Had it changed? Dense pines climbed higher along the ridge steps of the mountain, and for the first time since she'd showed up this morning, comfort warmed through him. He'd been all over the world as a Green Beret to distract him from what he'd left behind, but when his chips had been cashed in after the ambush that'd killed his unit, there'd only been one place left to go. Home. "Especially tourists."

"Because of what happened a couple months ago?" Her voice softened, and the hollowness behind his rib cage revolted. "The way you reacted before…when your hands were shaking… You said you'd been involved in the investigation, but it was more than that, wasn't it? You were buried, too."

Easton ripped the steering wheel to the right. He

slammed on the brakes, throwing them both forward in their seats, as the truck came to a sudden stop. He shoved the pickup into Park. Dust kicked up in front of the hood and blocked out the view of the road. His pulse rocketed into dangerous territory as he prepared for the onslaught of memory and pain. "What the hell are you doing, Genevieve? You show up at my cabin after all these years, and you think because we have a past that gives you the right to pry into my life? You don't know me. You don't know what I've been through or who I've lost. You made it pretty clear you wanted nothing to do with me when you left, so why start now?"

Shocked silence descended between them, and her mouth parted slightly.

Easton struggled to contain the repressed rage he'd carried all these years. He forced himself to take a deep breath, but the pain was always there. Always close to the surface.

"You're right. You don't owe me anything. I'm sorry. I thought…" She shook her head as though the simple action could rewind time, and a wave of shame increased its grip on him. She hugged her overnight bag closer to her. "We don't have to talk about anything other than the case. It won't happen again."

He pried his grip from the steering wheel and let his palms slide to the bottom. The dust cleared, revealing serrated peaks fighting to pierce the bright blue sky. A herd of deer stared back at the truck from their position a few yards away. The soft call of a crystalline river flowed alongside the dirt road before it widened into the impossibly green-blue lake taking over the small valley after this year's snow. So different than the bare, blood-soaked, dust-bowl dunes of Afghanistan. Easton pressed his lower back into the peeling plastic seat. Damn it. He'd nearly managed to move past these spurts of rage and isolation with the help of Weston and his parents, but there was no denying he'd ever had control when it came to Genevieve.

But that had never been her fault.

"It's not because of what happened during that case. The…" He ground his back teeth as another flood of shame rose to suffocate him. "The shaking. Weston and I, we were buried in a freezer barely big enough to contain the two of us, but the flashbacks and the bouts of anger started long before then."

She centered that watery mesmerizing gaze on him, and his heart tapped double time. Hell, his mother and Weston, even his father, had gotten used to seeing him like this, but he'd never intended to expose himself for the bitter bastard he really was. "How long?"

"Since my discharge." Easton compressed the brake to counter the buildup of energy streaking down his legs, and the cabin of his truck suddenly seemed so much…smaller than a minute before. "I was the only one in my unit who made it home after our caravan was hit by an IED during our last mission."

Her mouth parted on a strong exhale as though his words had physically hit her. Sunlight breached through the passenger side window and haloed around her from behind, softening the outline of her face. Genevieve stretched one hand out, sliding long fingers across his thigh, but thought better of touching him and pulled away. Too soon. "I'm sorry. I had no idea."

"Why would you?" His nerve endings protested at the loss of her touch, but it was only his imagination. The connection they'd had didn't exist anymore. She hadn't come to him to make up for the past. She'd showed up on his doorstep to ask for his help with a case. That was it. They weren't friends. They didn't keep in touch. He was the best chance she had of outwitting whoever had killed her assistant. Nothing more. Easton notched the pickup into Drive and pulled back onto the road.

The engine revved higher as he topped the first hill before the landscape dipped and spread out into another valley. He turned the shuddering truck once more up a long dirt drive. Two massive logs supporting the sign over the entrance to the fenced property reading Whispering Pines Ranch stood at attention as they passed underneath. Unsteady ground threatened to slow them down as they drove toward the main cabin ringed by the tree line. The cabin's green roof and trim set the structure apart from the six smaller satellite cabins located less than a few hundred yards in each direction. It wasn't much, but it was home.

Easton maneuvered the truck closer to his cabin and parked in nearly the same spot Genevieve had this morning. It'd only been six hours since he'd laid eyes on her after all these years, but so much had changed. He'd never talked about his time overseas, about the terror he'd witnessed or the side effects of losing his unit, but he'd opened up to her. Why? He reached for her arm as some unknown need drove him to keep her in the truck a little bit longer. "Genevieve."

She turned to face him, her hand settled over the door latch.

Years of imagined conversations, confrontations and accusations vanished the longer he studied her. She'd broken his heart. One day decided she'd had enough of him and this town, everything they'd built together, and disappeared. It hadn't been until he'd recognized her on the news a couple years ago when she'd been prosecuting a big case that he'd even realized where she'd gone. Her sweater gave under a single stroke of his thumb and drew her gaze to his hand. Fire burned up his spine as her pupils dilated, nearly blocking out the ring of color in her irises. Easton cleared his throat, peeling his fingers from around her arm. "I need to make sure it's safe before you go in."

"You think he could've followed us?" Genevieve settled back into her seat.

"No, but the second my mother realizes you're here, she might run you out of town with her rifle. Better to be safe than sorry." He shouldered out of the pickup and slammed the door behind him, cutting off the slight comfort of her warmth and perfume. What the hell had he been thinking bringing her out here? His family was barely recovering from his father's death at the hand of a killer, and he'd immediately thought to bring another to their door. His hand tingled with the memory of how her sweater had felt against his skin, and Easton curled his fingers into a fist as he rounded the hood of the truck. There was something very wrong with him.

The last tourist of the weekend had checked out this morning, but he still felt the need to knock before pushing inside the cabin a few yards from his. As though he expected the killer to answer back. Easton pressed his toes into the wooden door as he turned the knob. The scent of wood smoke and cured meat burned down his throat.

The space didn't allow for more than the single counter space off to his left, a small kitchen table straight ahead with two chairs, a single beaten love seat at the back near the fireplace and a twin-sized bed shoved in the corner, but it'd be enough. Looked as though his mom had already been through to make the bed, empty the trash can and wash the dishes. There wasn't anything else here to distract him from the woman waiting for him outside in the truck.

Nothing but a killer determined to claim her for himself.

Chapter Four

She'd run out of tape.

Despite Easton's warning that her murder board art project wouldn't fit inside the cabin, she'd set out to prove him wrong. And failed. The cabin was everything she remembered and everything she wanted to forget. Cozy, secure, full of memories. Each of the Ford boys had gotten their own cabin when they'd turned eighteen if they wanted to live and work on the ranch. This one had been Easton's.

Of course, this had to be the one he'd put her up in for the night.

Genevieve pressed the tape dispenser teeth into her thumb. No word from the police chief or the coroner who'd taken custody of the ear yet. They had no idea where the dismembered ear had come from, who'd sent it or if the Contractor had butchered another victim. She was still waiting for the report from the Alamosa medical examiner concerning Elisa Johnson's autopsy, but even then, Captain Morsey had banned her from looking into the case. Without access to updates concerning the most recent murder file, all she had was what she'd managed to bring with her. She focused on the spread of case files in front of her, but her gaze kept drifting out the window toward the cabin next door. It wasn't enough Easton had showed up at her motel room a few hours ago offering to help with the investigation, but he'd brought her to his family ranch. The epicenter of what her future would've looked like if she'd stayed.

The reverberation of footsteps echoed from the front door before two light knocks registered. Easton. Two steps and she'd crossed the kitchen and twisted the old ornate brass doorknob. Massive shoulders and a hint of soap consumed her senses as he filled the doorway, and her legs shook at the thought of collapsing into him. She wasn't exactly sure how much time had passed since she'd found Elisa strung up from her living room ceiling, but she hadn't slept. Hadn't eaten. None of which she could blame on anyone other than herself. "Hi."

"I brought you something." He held up a package of Scotch tape, unopened.

"You've been reading my mind." Genevieve buried her face in her palms, forgetting she still held the tape dispenser, and stabbed herself between the eyes. Stinging pain lightninged across her skin. She let go of the tape dispenser and pressed her hand to her head, coming away with a light streak of blood. "Ow, damn it."

His deep laugh grazed along her nerve endings and burrowed through sore muscle, straight into bone. It battled the fear undermining her thoughts and swept the doubt lodged in her chest clear. "Here. Let me."

Easton maneuvered around her, larger than life, and went straight for the cabinet under the sink to her left. He pulled out a first-aid kit and popped it open on the counter.

"It's fine." This was ridiculous. She didn't need a first-aid kit for a scratch of her own making. "You don't have to—"

"I know." His voice softened. "But we should at least clean it to prevent it from getting infected. Small wounds like this can turn into big problems if you're not careful." He ripped open an alcohol pad and centered himself in front of her. "Hold still. This is going to sting." Raising his hand in front of her face, he stroked the cold pad across her forehead. Sea-blue eyes steadied on the work in front of him.

"Did you learn that while you were deployed?" As much as she hated the thought of seeing him nearly break down in front of her at the motel, there was a deep need to know what he'd been through.

What he'd survived. It wasn't enough a killer had used her assistant to punish her. She'd moved on to punishing herself by leaning into the temptation surrounding him.

"You learn a lot in a combat zone." His gaze lowered to hers, his movements more controlled, hesitant. As though he was preparing for another fight, but the last thing she wanted was to walk back into his life and mess everything up for him again. "Not sure I've ever had to clean a wound from a plastic tape dispenser though."

"Guess there's a first time for everything." Her laugh escaped past her lips, full and genuine. A first in a long time. She held still, cataloging the differences in his expression from over the years. He was older, of course, with lighter threads of hair at his temples. The cleft in his chin seemed more pronounced, but not in a bad way. He'd stopped using gel to style his hair, letting it lie where it fell. Thick bands of muscle roped his arms as he peeled a Band-Aid from the wrapper and gently pressed it to her forehead. Overall, he'd exemplified the best of his gene pool, but there was a weight—almost a shadow—in the way he concentrated on her that hadn't been there before. Experience. Wisdom. Trauma?

He smoothed the edges of the Band-Aid against her skin, rough calluses catching on the fabric. "There. Good as new."

"Thank you." She couldn't remember the last time someone had gone out of their way to take care of her like this. It was nice. It was…warm. Something she'd missed since turning her back on Battle Mountain. And him. Genevieve cleared her throat as he seemed to linger on setting the bandage. "Any word from Weston about the shipping warehouse?"

Reality penetrated the bubble they'd inadvertently created around themselves, and Easton set about cleaning up the wrapper pieces. "He interviewed everyone who'd been on shift this morning. No one remembers seeing anything or anyone out of the ordinary. Weston's running background checks on all of the employees to be thorough, but as of right now, it's looking like a dead end."

"What about the surveillance footage?" Such a simple question, but the entirety of this case hinged on them finding something they could use to identify the Contractor. Anything.

"Disabled about ten minutes before the first shift started loading the trucks," he said.

"Which means he knew their schedule, knew where the cameras were." Genevieve pressed one hand to her forehead, igniting the sting under the bandage he'd set. No matter which angle they looked at this—from the first murder, the last or the package she'd received—the killer was one step ahead of them. Maybe more. "And the 9-1-1 recording of

Maria Gutierrez? Any chance Alamosa PD is willing to share with you?"

"I put in a call to Captain Morsey over there to get a copy, but once he learned one of his guys forwarded me the original case files, he severed contact. Seems there are unwritten rules that keep us from stepping into another department's investigation unless a body drops in our jurisdiction. He's holding any more information close to the chest." Easton tossed the bandage wrappers and settled himself against the arm of the couch, casual, at ease and home. "However, Chloe was able to get autopsy results for each of the victims from the medical examiner over there, and you were right. It's clear from the report on the fourth victim, Kayleigh Winters, that she was killed with a different size drill bit. The Contractor used a 5/16th, while whoever killed Winters used a 3/8th. That, combined with the wrong positioning of some of the steel eyelets the killer screwed into the victim's joints says we're very likely looking at two different killers."

"Corey Singleton killed Kayleigh Winters. He wanted her death to look like the work of the Contractor. He tried to put her murder on a serial killer to throw off suspicion. Only he didn't have the knowledge, the methodology or all the details that went into the kills." And she hadn't seen it. Not until it was too late for Elisa. Genevieve balanced against the kitchen table and stared out the window. "I knew there was something different about that case. I knew something wasn't right about Kayleigh's death, but I pushed ahead because I was so determined to stop the Contractor from killing again. Instead, I pissed off a serial killer, and Elisa Johnson ended up paying the price for my mistake."

"It wasn't your mistake, and this isn't your fault." Easton's boots reverberated off the hardwood floor and up through her heels as he closed the distance between them. "You're the prosecutor. You went to law school to protect the innocent and uphold the law. You aren't at the crime scenes. You aren't the one cutting into them to figure out how they died. You are not responsible for what happened to those women, Genevieve. The man who killed them is, and he'll pay for what he's done. You'll make sure of it."

She secured her arms around her midsection. Four victims. Four lives ended too early. "I've been trying to remember everything from when he was in my house. Anything that might tell us who he is, but all I can see is Elisa's face. I'd walked in the front door, and it looked as though she'd just been standing there, waiting for me. Every time I close my eyes, she's who I see." Genevieve swiped at her face to keep herself together, but it was no use. She hadn't been strong enough to fight off her attacker. What made her think she was strong enough not to fall apart? She raised her gaze to his. "It should've been me. Why wasn't it me?"

"I'm not sure I'm qualified to answer that for you. I've been asking myself that for over a year." The deep color of his eyes intensified the longer he stared at her, and in that moment, they seemed to reach a mutual understanding. One of loss, survival, guilt and pain. He'd lost his entire unit in a matter of seconds, walking away as the only survivor, and a killer had left her alive as punishment for not seeing his game for what it was. "We'll find him, Genevieve. Sooner or later, he's going to make a mistake. Killers like this get cocky believing they're out of reach. He's going to show his hand, and we'll be there to take him down."

"How? Alamosa PD isn't going to hand over that recording of the Contractor's first victim." She swiped the back of her hand under her eyes again and straightened, a fraction more stable than a few minutes ago. She wasn't sure why other than she wasn't alone. Despite what she'd done by leaving all those years ago, Easton was prepared to see this through to the end. "All we have is a theory about Maria Gutierrez knowing the killer, and detectives couldn't narrow down a suspect in the other three investigations. The only reason I was able to charge Corey Singleton with all four murders is because the

MOs matched. The cases are closed. The evidence is in storage, and we don't have access to any of it."

A smirk tugged at the corner of his mouth. "Captain Morsey might not be willing to share evidence, but I think I know someone who can get us that recording."

BATTLE MOUNTAIN'S POLICE station wasn't anything much. Weathered red brick that'd seen better days stacked two stories high to match the roofline of Hopper's Hardware attached on the other side. A low-key sign reading Police in blue lettering had only recently started lighting up again in part because of the improvements Weston had been making. The wild shrubs and a small section of uncut grass out front would be next on his list, Easton was sure.

The pickup's brakes squealed as he maneuvered into the parking lot off the back. The alleyway along the side of the building fed directly onto Main Street, giving a once staffed department easy access to main roads. A lot had changed in five years. The town's former police chief had done what he could to ensure his officers had employment here in town, but after the mines had shut down and the money had dried up, reserve officers had to move elsewhere. Leaving Charlie Frasier to patrol Battle Mountain for close to two years alone. Until he'd had a heart attack in the middle of a call.

Now Weston held the reins and called the shots.

Well, Weston, Easton and their dispatcher, Macie. Together they'd served and protected this town against one of the most motivated killers he'd ever met, including the hostile forces he'd faced overseas.

Easton shouldered out of the truck and rounded the hood, waiting for Genevieve to meet him before going inside. "Welcome home. Is it everything you remembered?"

"Worse." Doubt settled into the fine lines branching from the corners of her eyes, but when it came to plugging into the lifeblood of nearby departments, Macie Barclay was their only shot.

Genevieve watched her step on the crumbling cement stairs leading up the back of the station. Swinging open the glass door emblazoned with the department's shield etched in gold, she stepped inside. "The last time I was here, we'd gotten picked up by Chief Frasier for parking up at the lake. Your mother picked us up. I'd never been so embarrassed in my life."

"Can't lie. Those were some good times." Easton let the door close behind them and motioned her down the long stretch of old industrial carpeting. Burnt coffee assaulted his senses as they passed the two cells—both empty—and followed the narrow hallway to the front of the station. Another glass door let in the waning light as the sun slowly dipped behind the mountains and highlighted the two-level desk serving as the first stop for townsfolk.

A waterfall of red hair and thick citrusy perfume introduced the woman behind the desk. Macie Barclay turned kohl-lined eyes on them and flashed one of the whitest and widest smiles in existence. "Well, look what the cat dragged in. Your brother's not here, if that's why you've decided to grace us with your grumpy presence." Her gaze cut to Genevieve a split second before she bounced out of her chair. The dispatcher stretched a freshly manicured hand—so fresh Easton could still smell the nail polish through her perfume—to introduce herself. "Oh, you brought a friend. You're not from here. I'm Macie. Let me guess." Macie leaned back slightly, extending one long index finger. "You're a Libra."

"I'm sorry?" Genevieve accepted Macie's hand, her smile faltering.

"She means your astrological sign." Easton swallowed the urge to roll his eyes. They were here to play nice, and to play nice with Macie meant buying into whatever new subject she was obsessed with that week. From the study of volcanoes, to viruses and… what had she talked about for nearly an hour a couple weeks ago? Right. Three-hundred-year-old flowers kept in the Natural History Museum in London. With photos. Today, it looked like they were going to get their signs read.

"Oh," Genevieve said. "To be honest, I'm not sure. My birthday is the beginning of October."

"I knew it. Libra it is." Macie slid her hand from Genevieve's and took her seat with her pen pointed straight at the prosecutor. "You're beautiful, like to see every side of a topic, prone to fantasies and hate being alone." She turned caramel-colored eyes onto Easton as though she intended to wish him away. "Guess that explains why you're with the inspiration behind the middle finger."

"Is this about what I said?" Easton asked. "I don't believe this. All I said was that three-hundred-year-old plants aren't my thing—" He stopped himself cold. "You know what, we don't have to like the same things to work together, and that's not why we're here." He took a deep breath. "Macie, I need a favor."

"Wouldn't imagine you were here for a social visit." The dispatcher lowered her voice in a mock whisper to Genevieve. "It's a miracle the staleness of his cabin hasn't killed him yet."

Genevieve's laugh intensified the heat rising up his neck.

This was going well. "Do you know who the dispatcher is over in Alamosa?"

Macie focused on him. "Sure. Can't say we're friends considering she's been trying to get me to let her and her boyfriend use my treehouse for one of these weekends, but we're on speaking terms. Why?"

"We need the recording of a 9-1-1 call placed by a woman named Maria Gutierrez. Dispatch received the call two weeks before she was found murdered in her home. We think that call might tell us who killed her." Genevieve handed off the call logs she'd pulled from her file with the highlighted line. "We've asked the captain for a copy, but he doesn't want any other departments involved in the case."

Macie sat a bit straighter, the humor draining from her expression. She centered her gaze on Easton. "You're asking me to break department regulations, Easton. Alamosa's dispatcher could lose her job if Captain Morsey realizes you're working one of his cases, and Weston would take the heat if this connected back to us. What's going on?"

"We believe Maria Gutierrez's killer has butchered three other women, including Genevieve's assistant three days ago." There was no other way to stress the importance of that phone call. All the forensics, the autopsy reports, all the crime scene analysis—none of it had pointed back to their killer. "He broke into Genevieve's home, Macie. He strung Elisa Johnson from the ceiling for her to find, and there's a possibility she's next. I'm not going to let that happen, but I can't find him if I don't know who I'm looking for. Please."

He settled his hand over Genevieve's, leaning into her warmth.

The dispatcher's maroon-lipsticked mouth twitched below the light birthmark on the right side. Macie's gaze slid to Genevieve then back. "All right, but if you get caught, I'll say you used your woman's voice to imitate me and asked for the recording yourself. Understand?"

"Thank you." Relief crushed through him, but he wasn't willing to let go of the woman at his side.

"Don't thank me yet." Macie turned back to her desk and set her headset. She rapidly pecked a series of numbers Easton didn't recognize with the end of her pen and leaned back in her chair. "Valerie, hey. It's Macie over in Battle Mountain. Were you still interested in my treehouse this weekend?"

In less than five minutes, Macie's email pinged with an incoming download from Alamosa's dispatcher. "This better be worth it. The last time I let someone stay in my treehouse, I had to throw away my sheets. If your victim doesn't say her killer's name on this recording, I'm going to make you listen to another two hours of what other kinds of anemones the Natural History Museum keeps in their drawers. By the time I'm done, you'll love them as much as I do."

"I'd rather go back to Afghanistan." Easton leaned down and anchored both hands on the edge of the dispatcher's desk.

Genevieve elbowed him in the ribs.

Macie hit the white triangle positioned under a linear countdown of the recording. "Here we go."

The countdown ticked down. Background static punctured through the silence. "9-1-1, what is your emergency?" Another few seconds slipped by. "Hello, is anyone there?"

"Yes. I'm here." The woman on the other end of the line sounded calm, collected. Nothing like Easton had imagined if their theory the victim had known her killer was valid. "My name is Maria Gutierrez. I'm calling because I think…" Maria inhaled sharply, lowering her voice. Because someone else was in the house? "I think my friend might hurt someone."

Easton raised his gaze to Genevieve's. She'd been right. Maria Gutierrez must've known her killer and paid the price for that knowledge.

"Where is your friend now, ma'am?" the dispatcher asked on the recording.

"He's… I don't know. I… I don't know what to do. I didn't know who else to call." Shuffling reached through the background of the call as the victim paused. "He's exhibiting all the signs I was trained to watch for. He's been lying to me. He's manipulative, and he's growing more hostile. The smallest things are setting him off, and I'm not sure I can do this."

"Ma'am, are you in danger?" The dispatcher's keyboard penetrated through the line. "Can you get somewhere safe until an officer arrives?"

Maria dropped her voice to a whisper. "I think he knows."

The call ended.

Tension intensified the ache at the base of Easton's skull as he stared at the screen. Prying his grip from the edge of the desk, he turned to face Genevieve. His heart threatened to beat out of his chest. He wasn't sure what he'd expected to hear, but the fear in the victim's voice had unnerved him more than being locked inside a freezer with his brother. "You were right. She knew him. She knew what he was capable of and called 9-1-1 because she was worried that he was going to hurt someone."

"Macie, are you able to see if an officer was dispatched to Maria Gutierrez's home or if there was report detailing what happened after the call?" Genevieve diverted her attention to the computer screen.

The dispatcher swung her legs out from under the desk. "No. The only system I have access to is Battle Mountain's. If you want to see any incident reports, you'll have to go through Alamosa's captain."

"She saw the signs." A hint of that same fear Maria exhibited on that call settled in Genevieve's voice and raised the hairs on the back of his neck. "He was there. He figured out what she suspected."

Easton straightened. "And he killed her for it."

Chapter Five

The tremble in Maria Gutierrez's voice echoed in her head.

Genevieve shuffled through the stack of case files she hadn't gotten around to taping on the walls. Night had fallen, closing in tighter than she wanted to admit, as she huddled near the cabin's fireplace. Every light in the room cast a haloed glow to counter the shadows, but it wasn't enough to erase Maria's voice from playing on an endless loop.

The victim's smiling face stared back at her from the murder board. No matter how many times she'd gone through the case, there wasn't anything new. Detectives had run down acquaintances, coworkers, family members, friends and neighbors even remotely connected to Maria Gutierrez. Men and women alike. No arrest records or priors. No sealed juvie records detailing childhood hostility or experimentation on animals. Not one of the victim's friends or family members reported any new men in Maria's life, no one she was dating at the time. Nothing that would make them think she was in danger. The man who'd killed Maria had slipped into her life unnoticed and slipped right back out. A ghost.

Genevieve closed the file and stared into the flames in the fireplace. Her fingers tingled with the urge to toss the case file and all the others into the fire, to forget. Alamosa PD had closed their case. A killer was behind bars. The families had gotten the closure they'd deserved. Why couldn't she? The Corey Singleton case had shot her career forward more so than any other she'd prosecuted. Only now she realized, it'd all been based on a lie. She closed her eyes, exhaustion increasing gravity's hold on her body. There wasn't anything more she could do tonight. They'd found proof Maria Gutierrez had known her killer, but that didn't give them a name or a connection to the man who'd broken into Genevieve's house three nights ago. They were back to square one.

It seemed as though the floor rose to embrace her. She wasn't sure how long she lay there, warmed by the fire, safe. It wasn't just the cabin. As much as she'd feared coming here would raise the past from the dead, there was no other place she'd rather be. Whispering Pines had been her second home for so long, she'd left a part of herself here. The missing piece of her identity was here. Easton was here, and an easiness she'd never achieved outside of Battle Mountain slid through her.

The jolt of steady footsteps kept her in that purgatory space between sleep and wakefulness, and then she was floating. The hardness of the floor slid out from under her, and a shiver crossed her shoulder from the loss of heat. Strong arms secured her against a broad chest. Her fingers dug into soft cotton. So familiar.

"Damn it, woman, you look like death. When was the last time you ate something?" His voice rumbled straight through her, soothing the rough edges of doubt and fear strangling her from the inside.

"*You* look like death." Her accusation elicited a delirious laugh she couldn't contain. Okay, it might've been a while since she'd let herself slow down, but she'd pulled all-nighters before. She just needed a power nap. Then she could get back to the case. Genevieve pried open her eyes, meeting the sharp angles of his jaw and the tendons in his neck. Easton. The cabin dissolved around the edges of her vision. Her feet touched down on the twin bed positioned into the corner of the room before he slid her onto the mattress. Flannel blankets and crisp sheets brushed against her skin, and she sank deeper into the hug of familiarity and comfort. "I couldn't find him, Easton. The man who hurt Elisa. I tried, but he's too careful. How am I supposed to stop him if I don't know who he is?"

"By remembering you don't have to do it alone." Callused fingers brushed through the hair at her temple. The intensity in Easton's expression drained as he studied her, and her heart squeezed in her chest. "Chloe's been through the autopsy reports of the victims you attributed to the Contractor. Killers like him are compelled to follow their own set of rules. Deviating from those rules is rare. If we can find the pattern, we can find the connection between the victims. He chose them for a reason, Genevieve. Just as he chose you. They weren't random. We know Maria Gutierrez suspected what he was. We know he inserted himself into her life before killing her. It's possible he did the same with the others."

But would it be easy to prove? Would it be enough to find their killer? And did that mean a killer had inserted himself into her life, too?

The three lines between his eyebrows deepened. Only this time, she didn't fight the need to smooth them from existence. Reaching out, she skimmed her thumb over his forehead. Rough lines eased from his face, his breathing slowing, and the image of him in pain outside her motel room infiltrated into the moment. All her life, Easton Ford had been a rebellious hero in her eyes, out of reach, elusive, strong. But in that moment, he'd been…human, and she'd wanted nothing more than to deny she'd played a part in it. "Why are you doing this, Easton? Why are you still here after what I did?"

Seconds distorted into minutes, into what seemed like an hour as he raised that piercing gaze to her. He lowered his hand away from her temple, securing his fingers around her wrist. He pressed her skin to his. "Because I don't have anyone else."

The grogginess of running off three days' worth of adrenaline and minimal calories evaporated. She didn't understand. Genevieve pressed her free hand into the mattress and sat up to balance on her left hip. "What do you mean? You have your family. Your brother, your mom. They'd do anything for you, if you asked."

"They're not you." He pushed to his feet, turning his back on her. "The minute I returned home after my discharge, I knew something had changed. They started treating me differently, as if I was something that could be fixed given enough time. They keep their distance to give me my space. They avoid talking to me about what happened, waiting for things to just go back to normal. But there is no more normal. Not for me. They look at me with nothing but pity in their eyes, but you…" His voice dipped lower. "You look at me as though I'm the man you said yes to when I asked you to marry me, like I'm still the center of your world. Like I'm…whole."

Whole. She didn't know what to say to that, what to think. Genevieve slid her legs from beneath the covers, instantly aware she didn't have the protection of her jeans and sweater anymore. Instead, she'd changed into her sleep shirt and shorts when they'd gotten back to the ranch, completely exposed as she stood there in front of him. "Can I tell you a secret?"

The muscles in his throat constricted on his swallow. "Okay."

"None of us are whole." She stepped into him, setting her hand over his heart. "None of us get to walk away from this life without a few scars. Yes, yours are deeper. They're more violent. They've changed you and changed the course you thought your life would take, but you're still you. Out of all the people I could've gone to when I needed help, I knew I could depend on you."

He didn't answer.

"I'm not going to pretend to know what you've been through or how it felt when you realized you were the only one who'd survived that ambush. But to me, you're still every bit the man I think about before I close my eyes at night." The steady beat of his heart against her palm settled something in her. She didn't know how else to describe it other than peace. "You're the one who stepped between me and Adan Robinson when he wouldn't take no for an answer that day in the lunchroom. The one who called to make sure I was okay after you found the engagement ring and I'd already left Battle Mountain. You protected our country until they wouldn't let you back into the field again and immediately chose to defend this town as one of its reserve officers, and no one gets to see you as anything less than the brave, sacrificing, loyal man you are. Not even you."

Easton pressed his thumb into her palm. "None of that was good enough for you. Why would it be good enough for anyone else?"

"It was. It is. The day I left…" Her mouth dried as her own confidence cracked under his scrutiny. No. This wasn't about her. This wasn't the time or the place. "What I'm saying is you've always been there for me. No matter the situation or had badly I hurt you all those years ago, you never gave up on me. Now let me be here for you. To listen, to be in the same room as you, to read you a bedtime story—whatever you need from me. I'm here. I owe you that much."

"Would you really read me a bedtime story?" he asked.

The pressure behind her sternum released, and she couldn't hide the curl at the corner of her mouth. He swept his hand down her forearm, igniting a trail of goose bumps, before settling it under her elbow and tugging her closer. "I mean, I'm not going to read you the articles from a dirty magazine, but I'm sure we could work out some kind of arrangement."

"Nobody reads the articles in dirty magazines. No matter what they try to tell you." His exhale brushed against her neck as he drew her closer. He threaded his fingers into her hair at the base of her neck, and her heartbeat ticked up a notch.

The heat she'd lost when he carried her from her position in front of the fireplace reignited under the weight of his study. The investigation, the package she'd received at the motel, the terror that'd become part of her—none of it seemed real in the circle of his arms.

Easton strengthened his grip on her and lowered his mouth to hers.

THERE HADN'T BEEN anyone else.

Easton penetrated the seam of her lips. Hints of toothpaste and something sweet burst across his tongue as he memorized her from the inside out. Her lips were smooth and warm. His heart seemed to seize in his chest. The guards he'd kept in place to keep him from hurting the people around him cracked under pressure. Passion built in a tornado of heated frenzy until every cell in his body begged him for release, and he drew back to catch his breath.

Color infused the tops of her cheeks and ringed her lips. "Wow, that was…"

"Not exactly the reason I came over here." His fingers dimpled the skin of her arms. Damn, she felt good. Familiar and warm. He couldn't remember the last time he'd let himself disappear into uncertainty like that, that he'd felt that at peace. His pulse pounded out of control, but he feared if he let himself fall back into her, he might never surface. Genevieve had left him once, and the only way he'd survived was drowning himself in service to his country. There were no guarantees he'd make it through a second time. Because she would leave. Once this case was finished, she'd go back to her life in Alamosa. She'd forget all about him. Flames crackled from the fireplace, ripping him back into the moment. The woman who had the ability to anchor him in the storm of his own mind had become a target. He couldn't afford to forget that. Easton peeled his hands from around her arms. He cleared his throat.

"I was going to say intense." Her coy smile ignited another knot of desire. But no matter how long they tried to convince themselves reality didn't exist, it would come back to bite them harder than before if they weren't careful.

"Yeah. I guess I had a few things I needed to work out," he said.

"With my mouth." She laughed, a light compelling

note of music he'd fought to bury, but he'd only been kidding himself. "And you came over because…"

"Right. You've been running off of fumes since the attack. I thought I would take a look at your files while you rested. The ones I received from Alamosa PD aren't complete as far as I can tell, and the FBI is sandbagging me since I wasn't involved in the original case." He caught a whiff of the dinner he'd smuggled out of the main house. "Oh, and I brought you some of Mom's chili."

"I'm starving." She nearly lunged for the steaming bowl of hamburger, tomato, cheese and onions. Framing her fingers around the ceramic bowl, she inhaled the spicy aroma and raised curious green eyes to meet his. "You added pickles. I can't believe you remembered."

"I remember everything about you," he said.

She hauled a massive spoonful of chili into her mouth and closed her eyes, and damn, if that wasn't one of the most beautiful sights he'd ever seen. Despite the pain lodged under his rib cage, Genevieve had always captivated everyone around her like this. "I thought I'd made up how good her chili was, but it's heaven. Her homemade pickles are the best. Thank you."

"You're welcome." He circled the ring of papers she'd created in the center of the floor. Brightly colored sticky notes angled across multiple pages with handwritten notes. Witness statements had been highlighted, forensic test results compared between cases. She'd been at this for hours. "Anything new?"

"Not yet." Her spoon clinked against the side of the bowl as she maneuvered into his personal space. Pale skin warmed under the glow of the fire, but her gaze had lost the brightness he'd noted a few minutes before. "I've been through everything, including the victims' financials to try to connect them that way. There's a reason he chose these four women as a whole. I'm just not seeing it. They look nothing alike. Two of them visited the same restaurant the weeks they were killed, but that leaves two others who didn't. None of them were related or worked in the same fields. Apart from the fact they all lived in Alamosa or just outside city limits, there's nothing here to tell me why they were targeted."

"Well, the 9-1-1 recording told us Maria knew him. She was around him long enough to notice the signs something wasn't right. She called police because she feared he'd hurt someone." He bent to pick up the photo of Maria Gutierrez and straightened. "My guess, he killed her out of pure survival. She caught on to him before he could go after who he really wanted, so building a connection between her and the other three victims wouldn't get us far."

"You're saying she wasn't an intended target." Genevieve studied the arrangement of files around her feet. She set her bowl on the fireplace mantel and speared her fingers through her hair. "That would mean the FBI profilers based their initial assessments off of wrong information. They specifically built that profile based off of her when they took over after the second victim was found and tried to make the pieces fit when he killed the others."

"He told you Elisa Johnson was killed because of his disappointment in you," Easton said. "This isn't about finding a connection between the victims. We need to look at each case as its own crime. We need to find out what it was about each of these women that fascinated the killer."

"And we'll find him." Genevieve shifted her weight between both feet. "Okay. We know why Maria Gutierrez was killed. He didn't want her to expose him before he was ready. Friends and family don't know about any new men in her life, which means he made sure to keep a low profile. Elisa Johnson died because she had a connection to me. He didn't know her. He used her to get my attention." Her voice hitched on the last word, but she pushed on. She curled her index finger around her chin, and Easton caught a glimpse of the fire she'd lost since the attack, the intensity he'd always admired. "That leaves the other two victims. Annette Scofield was an Alamosa PD rookie. She'd only been on the job a few days when her partner arrived at her home to pick her up for their shift and discovered the body."

"The second victim was a police officer?" Instinct prickled at the back of his neck. Easton rifled through the victim's file. Annette Scofield had just graduated from the academy, but instead of taking on crime in a larger city as most officers were wont to do, she'd returned to her hometown. "An unofficial FBI profiler, an assistant in the district attorney's office and a rookie officer." It was a theory, but it might give them the break they needed. "Tell me about the third victim."

Genevieve collected the last file and handed it to him. "Um, Ruby Wagner. Twenty-eight years old, single…" Her mouth parted slightly. "She was an EMT for the city."

That was the connection.

"She was someone who had police connections and was familiar with human anatomy. When the killer broke into your house, you said he wanted you to become the opponent he deserves." Easton set the corner of the file in his hand in the center of her chest. "What if he put the same expectation on these victims as he put on you?"

"He's choosing them because he wants them to stop him." A combination of relief and exasperation unbalanced her, and she settled back onto the arm of the couch. "The first three victims were discovered in their own homes. As far as the crime scene units were able to tell, there were no signs of a break-in at any of the victims' residences, either. But the killer put Elisa Johnson in mine. He's rebelling against his own MO."

"It's possible he's escalating. He could be choosing targets that present a unique challenge. Maria because she could see him coming, Ruby as an EMT who would've known how to defend herself when it counted and Annette as an armed police officer. But they weren't able to stop him from killing, so he's moved on to the district attorney herself, but this time he wanted to announce himself. He went through your assistant. He broke into your home. He had chosen to confront you because of the challenge it presented then left her body to motivate you and to take the bait. He's upping the stakes for the pure joy of showing us his power." Which put Genevieve in more danger than they'd originally believed. If the killer was murdering the subjects of his experiments, how long did that give her?

There had to be more here they weren't seeing. The man who'd strung up Genevieve's assistant would've contacted each of his opponents to throw down the challenge to stop him. So why hadn't they gone to the police? Why hadn't they reported the incidents? Unless, they hadn't realized they'd been invited to his sick game.

"And the ear he sent to my motel room?" Her voice shook. The rawness in her expression cut straight through him. She was exhausted, barely making it through the day. Even now, she tried to hide the tremor in her hand, but Genevieve couldn't hide from him. She'd never been able to. "What does that have to do with anything? Who did it come from?"

He didn't know, and a part of him didn't want to know the answer. Seemed after the first three murders, this killer was determined to prove the FBI profilers and Genevieve wrong on every account. Tears welled in her eyes as she stared into the flames, and he couldn't hold himself back anymore. Easton crossed to the couch and took a seat beside her. Sliding his arm around her hips, he tugged her into his lap. She buried her nose in the crook of his neck. Right where he needed her. "Chloe should have more information for us in the morning. Until then, you should sleep. There's nothing left for us to do tonight, but I can stay as long as you need."

"Thank you." She set her hand against his chest. "I promise to read you a bedtime story tomorrow."

"I'm going to hold you to that." His body turned heavy as the weight of the day infiltrated every muscle, tendon and bone, but he didn't dare move. Genevieve's breathing slowed after a few minutes as he studied the faces of the victims spread out in front of them. Clutching her closer, Easton set his head against the back of the couch and closed his eyes.

For the first time in years, he didn't have to imagine what it'd feel like to hold her again. He had the real thing. She was here, in his arms, alive.

Now all he had to do was keep it that way.

Chapter Six

Sweat built along her neck and arm.

Genevieve pried her head from the damp flannel beneath her. To find that damp flannel belonged to the man she'd never thought she'd see again. His mouth hung open, the deep rumble of his inhales burrowing through her. Sunlight pierced through the small window near the front door and sharpened the angle of his jawline.

He'd held her all night. Aside from the years of pain she'd caused and her promise to be there for him, he'd put her needs ahead of his own. Again. She skimmed the backs of fingers beneath his chin. How on earth had she walked away from a man like him?

A low sound caught in his throat as Easton stretched long legs in front of him. His jeans molded to powerful thighs beneath her, and he blinked a few times to sweep the night from his eyes. That mesmerizing gaze slowly slid to her, hesitation etched in his expression. "How long have you been watching me sleep?"

"Long enough to discover your secret." She liked this game, the one where she could make him squirm for a few minutes, and she got to see the unguarded and exposed ranch hand she'd fallen in love with all those years ago. "You talk in your sleep."

"No, I don't." He scrubbed his hand down his face. "And you can't prove it."

"You sure about that?" Genevieve reached down in front of the couch into her duffel bag. She curled her fingers around the phone she'd purchased on her way out of Alamosa and brought up the recording app. Hovering her thumb above the play button, she committed this moment to memory. "Would you care to amend your statement, Officer Ford?"

Pure panic washed across his face, and her heart shot into her throat. "Whatever I said, I was obviously asleep. It wouldn't be admissible in court, and I'll deny everything."

A burst of laugher rushed up her throat, and she tossed her head back. Genevieve hit Play. His sleep-addled voice ran through the exact location where he'd hidden his brother's favorite teddy bear as a kid between bursts of deep inhales. "If I go out there with a shovel and follow these directions, am I going to find Weston's Crunchy the Bear?"

Easton sat a bit straighter, which was harder to

manage with her still in his lap. "I can explain. He stole my collection of superhero cards to trade them at school with his friends. Hiding his bear was payback. That's all, and then… I might've forgotten Crunchy was still out there."

"Easton." She wiggled the phone in front of him.

"Okay. I didn't forget, but I warned him what would happen if he didn't get those cards back. I told him what I would do to that bear, and he didn't follow through. So, really, it's his fault," he said. "He's a grown man, a police chief, for crying out loud. I don't think he's still missing his bear."

His cell pinged with an incoming message.

She gripped the phone and set her feet to the cold hardwood floor. The fire had gone out hours ago, but she'd managed to sleep better than ever. Because of him. "You better hope not, or I'm going public."

"I'm going to get that recording." Easton lifted his hips off the cushion and retrieved his phone from his jeans. "Chloe has results on the ear that was sent to you at the motel room, but she's not comfortable talking about it unless it's face-to-face. I should get down there."

"I just need a few minutes to get ready." Genevieve collected a fresh set of clothes from her bag, but she was running out of clean outfits. Three days since leaving Alamosa, and all she had to show for it was unbridled fear threatening to rip her apart whenever she closed her eyes.

"I'm not sure that's a good idea, Genevieve." He'd lowered his voice, but every word registered as though he'd shouted across the room.

"It's not a good idea to get ready or that I come with you to see Chloe?" Halfway to the bathroom, clothes and toiletries in hand, she slowed. He didn't need to answer. It'd been clear in his tone. No. He didn't get to sideline her in the middle of the play. She turned to face him, her fingers aching from the grip on her belongings. "I brought you this case. Don't you think I should be the one to make the call whether or not I'm involved?"

"This killer challenged his victims to stop him before he screwed eyelets into their knees and elbows and anywhere else he could before he hung them from the ceiling with fishing line." He pointed a strong index finger toward the floor to enunciate his point, but all she heard was that blood-curdling doubt in his voice. "He's already broken into your home. He's made it clear you're his next obsession, and I can't protect you if you're not trying to protect yourself."

"And I can't make sure he pays for what he's done if you lock me in my room," she said. "What are you doing, Easton? Do you think because you kissed me, and we spent the night on the couch together, that

I'm going to let you do this without me? He might already have his next victim, and I'm not going to stand here and do nothing about it. You of all people should understand that."

"Do you want to end up like them?" The collapse of his defense took physical form as he stumbled back a step, and in that moment, she wasn't exactly sure which Easton she was talking to. The former fiancé, the soldier who'd survived Afghanistan or the Battle Mountain PD officer. "I can't..."

Seconds distorted between them.

They didn't have time for this. They'd made a connection between a killer and his prey, and they couldn't let that lead slip through their fingers. This was the first break in the case since Corey Singleton had copied the Contractor's MO, and she'd promised herself to see it through. The man who'd broken into her home wouldn't stop with her, but she had the chance to stop him. Here. Now. "You can't, what, Easton?"

"I can't lose you again!" He lunged forward, framing his hands on either side of her face. Fire burned in the depths of his eyes. His chest rose and fell in violent waves as he forced her back two steps. The hard length of his body pressed against hers. "I just got you back. Don't you understand that?"

She honed on the small muscles ticking below his jaw. Genevieve dropped her clothes at her feet, her toiletries spilling out of her cosmetics bag, but she didn't care. This moment. This was the one that had the potential to destroy the connection they'd started rebuilding, and she didn't want to lose that. She slid her fingers up his forearms, her senses at full attention. "The morning of our wedding, I was looking at myself in that dress in front of the mirror."

He moved to release her, but she kept his palms in place. "Genevieve—"

"No, you've been wondering what happened that day all these years. You deserve an answer." She forced herself to take a deep breath as the truth burned to the surface. "You were the reason we got together. You were the one always making sure I got to work okay and that I had everything I'd ever wanted for our wedding. You were this amazing, dedicated guy all the girls wanted, and I was nobody."

His mouth parted to argue, but she wouldn't let him.

"No one ever looked twice at me. Except you. I didn't understand why you'd stepped in between me and Adan Robinson that day in the lunchroom, or why you asked me out on the way home. I didn't know why you'd want me at all. Then the longer we were together, I realized I'd gotten so wrapped up in you and your personality, in this idea of what we looked like to everybody else, that when I finally faced myself in the mirror, I didn't know who I was anymore. My parents, my brother—they all loved you. They pushed me to make the leap. To marry you, have your babies, to help you run this ranch and create this big family legacy, because that's what I was supposed to do. For them, Battle Mountain was it. There wasn't anything outside of this town, but when I was in that dress, all I saw myself as was... yours. I've spent the past fifteen years trying to prove I'm my own person." She shifted her weight between both feet and licked her lips. "Please don't try to unravel my hard work."

She'd never said the words out loud before, wasn't sure if they made sense, but it was too late to take them back now. Understanding melted the intensity from his gaze, and the pressure behind her rib cage subsided. "My leaving had nothing to do with you. Okay? I needed to create my own identity, away from you and this town. But the truth is, you can't lose me again because I'm not that woman you knew. Not anymore."

He smoothed his thumbs across her cheeks. A hint of acceptance filtered across his expression, and he backed away. "I believe you, and I have no right to decide if you're involved in this case, but I'm still your partner during the course of this investigation. If there is any doubt about your safety, I'll do whatever it takes to keep you alive. Understand?"

"I understand." Genevieve collected her clothes and toiletries from the floor and held them close to her chest. Her skin tingled under the remnants of his touch as she turned toward the bathroom. "I'm going to get ready. I'll be a few minutes."

"I'll meet you at the truck. There's something I have do to." Easton headed for the front door of her small cabin, and before she had a chance to take her next breath, he was gone.

Genevieve closed the door behind her and set her belongings on the small countertop. After twisting on the shower, she stripped free of her pajama shirt and shorts. She could still smell him on her, that combination of soap and man, as though he'd seamlessly worked under her skin all over again. A single day. That was all it'd taken to fall back into Easton's gravitational pull, but she wasn't nineteen anymore. She was stronger than her basic instincts, and she'd walk away from the investigation every ounce the woman she'd worked to become. Even if it meant never seeing him again.

She scrubbed from head to toe with the lavender-scented soap provided to tourists staying at the ranch and washed his influence down the drain.

THE JACOB FAMILY FUNERAL HOME had become a poor substitute for the coroner's office the past few years, but there wasn't anywhere or anyone else in Battle Mountain willing to work with the dead.

Easton shoved the shuddering truck into Park out front. Residents took to Main Street on foot, coming and going through the old ma and pa shops that made up the heart of the town. Jagged cliffs and budding trees cast shadows along the street. But while a calm had settled over the town since a serial killer had claimed this area as his hunting grounds two months ago, a storm churned violently inside him.

He'd finally gotten the answer he'd been searching for since his wedding day. Genevieve had disappeared because she'd needed to figure out what she'd wanted to do with her life, to break away from the expectations of his family, hers, this town. She'd wanted more than he'd been able to offer at the time, more than him. Hell if he didn't blame her, but knowing the answer didn't lessen the loss he'd sustained or make it any less real.

"This is the coroner's office?" Genevieve pushed out of the truck, a few strands of hair sticking to the coat of intense red lipstick. She swiped at her face as she studied the two-story facade.

Easton followed and slammed the driver's side door behind him. A low whistle cut down the canyon. The official town anthem. "Chloe has an office set up in the back. Morbid, but it does its job."

He motioned her ahead of him before ascending the three short steps inside.

Cool air tainted with a hint of cleaning chemicals dove into his lungs. Neutral walls and industrial carpet that'd once been littered with shattered glass from a bullet meant for Weston and Chloe had been replaced with a darker color. Images of the last time he'd stepped through this door threatened to pull him out of the moment, but he wasn't here to relive the past. It'd moved on without him. Easton led them through the sales room and deeper into the building.

Dr. Chloe Miles's office wasn't more than a single room with an exam table in the center, a drain underneath and an L-shaped formation of white cabinets stocked with medical supplies. No bodies today. Well, not entirely. He knocked on the open door, and the coroner turned with a wide smile. "You said you had some information on the ear sent to Genevieve yesterday morning?"

"Yes, come in. I don't…really have anywhere for you to sit though." Chloe's long dark hair had been pulled back in a tight bun at the nape of her neck. Her white lab coat accentuated sandalwood skin and the myriad of freckles across the bridge of her nose. Somehow, his soon-to-be sister-in-law maneuvered around the room on heels as though she'd been born in them. "Your brother borrowed my stool and never brought it back."

"The counter is fine." Easton took the edge of one cabinet, off guard as Genevieve settled next to him. Her fingers brushed against his, and his blood pressure skyrocketed. He forced himself to focus. "Did you find anything that can tell us who sent the package yesterday?"

"The tests I ran on the box itself produced one set of partial fingerprints. I compared them against the driver who delivered the package and was able to eliminate him based on his driving route and his phone's GPS at the time the truck was loaded. He's not your guy." Chloe rounded the head of the exam table. "But I found another partial print permanently sealed under the label the killer used to make the package blend in with the others. Unfortunately, the label's adhesive is making it impossible for me to run it through the federal database, so I need to send it to Unified Forensics in Denver. Even then it might not be enough to get an ID."

"That could be the killer." Genevieve stepped forward, her gaze locked on the spread of flattened cardboard inside of an evidence bag on the table. "What about all the other employees at the shipping warehouse?"

"According to their statements to Chief Ford, they were all wearing gloves when they loaded that truck yesterday morning. He alibied them out one by one, and I was able to compare the prints I found to each one of them," Chloe said. "No dice."

"What about the ear itself?" Easton sensed the defeat coursing through Genevieve's shoulders and stepped into her side. Securing his hand at her lower back, he intended to provide comfort, but she stepped around the far edge of the table. Out of reach. He forced himself to breathe through the slight chemical smell seemingly soaked into the drywall. "From the amount of blood coagulated around this edge, whoever he took it from was still alive when he cut it off."

"You're right." Chloe snapped latex gloves over long fingers and turned the ear on its side, incision side up. "I've determined the ear was severed two to four hours before it was delivered to your motel room yesterday morning. I've run DNA without any hits in the system, but I can tell you the victim is female, approximately thirty to thirty-five years old based on the age of skin, Caucasian and had detached lobes. Other than that, there's not much here for me to go off of. If I had a complete skull or even a sliver of bone, a forensic anthropologist would be able to pull a chemical signature about the area the victim grew up in. With what we have, there are no piercings, scars or other identifying characteristics. Not even any evidence of diseases in the cartilage or blood, but…" The coroner slid her pinky into the ear's canal. "If you look closely, you can see an abnormal structure of the outer ear, in the dip here right before the canal."

Easton maneuvered to get a closer look opposite Genevieve on the other side of the table. He leaned in. "It's not natural?"

"I don't think so, no." Chloe laid the ear on the layer of disposable drape. "It's possible the ear formed around an ill-fitting hearing aid. Something the victim would've worn when she was younger and still growing. Based on the density of the malformation, I'd say she wore the device for most of her childhood, and the cartilage grew around it the older she got."

"A female victim, early to midforties, Caucasian with a hearing aid." Genevieve focused on the evidence, but he could've sworn there'd been a hitch in her voice. She cleared her throat. "You should get a hold of Captain Morsey from Alamosa PD. Run the details by him to compare to missing persons reports in the area."

Easton retrieved his phone but hesitated sending the info. Something wasn't right. He wasn't sure how else to put it. "If there's another woman out there, what's her role in the killer's game?"

"What do you mean?" Genevieve asked.

"We determined the victims Alamosa PD and the FBI found strung up from their ceilings were women he was grooming to rise to his challenge. Like you."

So why had the game suddenly changed? "Nothing in the previous files indicated he'd ever dismembered his victims or held them hostage. What makes this one so special?"

Genevieve slid her hands into her slacks. "You theorized he was escalating."

"Escalating usually means changes in frequency and violence. Not entire MO shifts." Although it wasn't unheard of, but that usually meant the killer was experimenting with his ritual and rarely followed a strict sequence of kills. No. This was a veteran killer. Organized, intelligent, careful. Easton messaged Alamosa PD's captain the details on their potential victim. There was more to this killer. An element they hadn't been able to uncover yet. Hell, even with Easton's up close and personal experience with the man who buried Chloe and Weston two months ago, he had a hard time cataloguing this killer. "This doesn't make sense."

"Well, until we get a positive ID from the partial print from Unified Forensics or a match to the ear's DNA, I've given you everything I have," Chloe said. "It's up to you to find him now."

"Thank you, Dr. Miles. You've been very helpful." Genevieve wound around the table and strode toward the door, faster than he expected. "Excuse me. I need to make a call."

One glance from his future sister-in-law told him

he'd better follow her out, and he nodded. "Thanks for your help."

He met a wall of fresh air as he shoved through the glass door and out onto Main Street. The chemical burn in his nose subsided, but the tension at the base of his skull refused to let up. He caught sight of Genevieve a few yards down the sidewalk, her back turned toward him. "Hey."

She turned at his approach, one hand pressed against her head. "Hey. I just had to get out of there."

"You're acting like severed body parts aren't part of your everyday routine." His sarcasm missed the mark. As a district attorney, she'd tried and prosecuted the worst criminals in southern Colorado, but studying the evidence from crime scenes and seeing it firsthand were entirely different things. The need to reach out to her, to settle the fear etched into her expression, tensed the muscles down his spine. But the way she'd pulled away from him in Chloe's office said no amount of comfort would wipe the agony swirling in her gaze. "Tell me what's going on."

"There's only one person I told I was leaving Alamosa three days ago, Easton, and now he has her." Genevieve jerked her arm down. "A woman in her early to midforties, Caucasian, hearing disorder."

His voice deadpanned. "You advised me to reach out to Alamosa PD's captain to run the details against any missing persons in the area. Because you knew."

"I tried calling her, but there's no answer. It keeps going to voicemail." Genevieve pressed the back of her hand holding her burner phone against her mouth, but a gut-wrenching sob still managed to escape. "I thought she'd be safe, but he must've followed me to her house. He must've seen me drive away in her car. He cut off her ear and sent it to me to let me know I wouldn't ever be able to escape him."

"The family member from one of your previous cases." Easton was already dialing. He pressed the phone to his ear as the line connected. "I need a name, Genevieve."

She swiped at her face. "Laila Ballard."

Chapter Seven

The truck protested the entire length of the drive.

Her fingers ached from gripping the edge of the old plastic seats until they hit Alamosa's town limits, but even then, she couldn't defuse the explosion of panic suffocating her from the inside. The three-hour drive stretched into days as they raced along the highway connecting Battle Mountain to the rest of the state, and still, it wasn't fast enough.

Patrol cars lined the street of the quiet neighborhood as they approached the house. Everything Genevieve remembered about the small rambler-style home looked the same as it had before she'd left town, but the entire world had changed. Beige stucco fractured along the base of the home where Laila Ballard had planted rose bushes of varying colors. Soggy leaves left over from winter overflowed from the gutters running the length of the roofline and fell to the wraparound porch styled with minimalistic outdoor furniture.

She and Laila had sat in those chairs and talked about her daughter's case countless times. How a drunk driver who'd been granted bail had once again gotten behind the wheel intoxicated. How he'd run a red light and plowed into the side of her daughter's car. Genevieve had kept her apprised of every development, and in the end, succeeded in making sure her child's killer had been punished. Now the mother who'd grieved her daughter's death had become a victim herself.

"Laila doesn't have any connection to law enforcement or experience with serial investigations. Her daughter was killed by a drunk driver last year. She's got nothing to do with this." Genevieve watched the police filter in and out of the home. EMTs had arrived on scene, but her gut told her Laila wasn't inside the house. There was no body because the killer still had her. Her stomach churned at the thought. First Elisa Johnson, now Laila Ballard. Seemed even the smallest connection put her associates and friends at risk. What did that mean for the man beside her? For her family? Colleagues?

"The crime scene unit is still going through the house. Captain Morsey won't let anyone near it until they're finished processing. If they find anything, we'll know. There's no way he can block us from getting involved now, not with the ear sent to you in Battle Mountain." Easton's voice penetrated through the wall of anxiety swelling in her throat, urging her to think logically and not emotionally. But this case was emotional. It was personal. "We're going to find him, Genevieve. I give you my word."

"How many other people will suffer before we do?" Storm clouds rolled over one another above, and within a few seconds rain hit the windshield and streaked down the passenger side window. Lightning shot across the sky, followed by the deep vibration of thunder. "How long until he turns his attention on everyone else I care about? What about you?"

"Hey." Warm hands coerced her to face him, and once she did, she met nothing but defiance in his expression. Easton tugged her across the seat, held her close, and she wanted nothing more than to stay in this moment of peace. "I've already got Weston moving your parents to a secure location and put word in with your office. Your brother should be fine now that he lives out of state. And you don't have to worry about me. Okay? I knew exactly what I was getting myself into when I showed up at your motel room yesterday. Just remember whatever happens, we do this together. Right?"

"Right." The promise in his voice, in his words, chased back the loneliness she'd tried denying ever existed since leaving Battle Mountain years ago. "But in case you die during this investigation, I want you to know I'm sorry."

His laugh drowned out the sound of the rain ticking in rhythm to her racing heartbeat. "I'll be sure to remember that."

"No." Genevieve sat up, locking her gaze on his. "I'm sorry. Whatever happens, I need you to know that."

Humor bled from his expression.

"You deserved better than me," she said.

He didn't move, didn't even seem to breathe. "Genevieve, I—"

Three loud raps on the passenger side window twisted her to confront the officer on the other side. Captain Morsey holstered his baton and stepped away from the truck to allow her room to get out. Tension bunched in her shoulders as she moved to open the door. Stark blue eyes remained on her as she slid from the vehicle. The truck rocked on its shocks as Easton did the same. Defined lines deepened in an aged face as Captain Morsey shifted his attention from her to Easton and back. They'd only met a couple of times—not enough to form a professional or personal relationship—and from the way he stared them both down, she imagined that was as far as they would go. The captain's hand hovered over his baton as he sized up the Battle Mountain PD officer rounding the hood of the truck. "Counselor." He nodded before speaking to Easton. "I take it you're the other Ford, Weston's brother."

"Yes, sir." Easton extended his hand in introduction, but the captain ignored the offering. "Anything you can tell us about Laila Ballard?"

"I don't know how you and your brother do things in the middle of nowhere, Ford, but I told you from the beginning. This is my case." Captain Morsey hiked his hands to his hips as he surveyed the scene. "Now, I know you folks are new to homicide investigation, but we have rules about other departments stepping on our toes. You're not needed here. My department has this well under control."

He had to be joking. Genevieve took a single step forward. "With all due respect, Captain. The man you arrested for the deaths of Maria Gutierrez, Annette Scofield and Ruby Wagner isn't the Contractor. He's still out there—"

"Ms. Alexander, your assistant was murdered and discovered hanging from the ceiling in your home three days ago. As of right now, I have grounds to have you arrested for leaving Alamosa as a person of interest and interfering in the investigation." The captain's voice dropped into dangerous territory. "I don't care who either of you are. Come near this case again, I will throw you in jail. Do you understand?"

She didn't know what to say, what to think.

Easton acquiesced. "Yes, sir."

"Good. Now, I got a missing woman to find, and I'd appreciate if you let me do my job." Captain

Morsey headed back toward the house, leaving them on the sidewalk as the storm protested overhead. He turned back. "Oh, and I'll be needing that ear your coroner examined. I'd rather have my medical examiner take a look. Until then, Lieutenant Parrish will make sure you get to wherever you're staying."

A younger version of the captain stepped into her peripheral vision, but Genevieve only had attention for the defeat coiling through her. They'd been barred from searching the scene of Laila Ballard's abduction, from examining any forensics the killer might've left behind and had officially lost the only piece of evidence linking Laila to their killer.

Strong fingers slipped beneath her arm as the lieutenant Captain Morsey had sicced on them tried to pry her away from the scene. "Let's go, Counselor."

Genevieve wrenched her arm out of the lieutenant's grip.

Before she had a chance to confront him herself, Easton stepped between her and the officer. "I don't give a damn who you work for, you don't get to touch her. Understand?"

Lieutenant Parrish's mouth ticked higher at one side, as though looking for the opportunity to follow through with Captain Morsey's threat to have them both arrested and put behind bars. The lieutenant raised both hands in surrender. "Just following orders, sir. I didn't mean anything by it."

"Come on." Easton secured his hand at her lower back and maneuvered her toward the passenger side door of his truck. "The storm is getting worse. We need to find a room for the night."

The weight of the lieutenant's attention tightened the muscles down her spine as she climbed back into the truck. He watched them pull away from the curb then headed for his own patrol car parked behind them. The back half of the vehicle remained in her side-view mirror as they wound through the city.

Rooted in the heart of the San Luis Valley, Alamosa offered everything from natural wonders and outdoor activities, to culture and authentic eats. The city's close proximity to sights and attractions made it an ideal spot for tourists summiting the country's tallest sand dunes, wrestling local alligators, chasing waterfalls and relaxing in the hot springs. It was the place she'd called home the minute she'd run from Battle Mountain. Only now the familiarity of these streets grated against her sense of belonging.

Genevieve let the view blur in her vision. Not focusing on anything in particular. "I'd invite you to stay in my guest room, but, as far as I know, my house is still officially a crime scene."

"A motel is fine." He took a sharp right into the parking lot of the Riverside Inn, a one-level stretch of brown stucco and iconic hacienda architecture. A massive tree planted close to the main road broke up the number of cars parked in the lot, and her gut clenched. Limited availability.

Lieutenant Parrish parked behind them as she and Easton shouldered out of the truck but didn't move to follow. Genevieve studied him through the windshield with help from the dim lights outside each motel room door. She stuck her tongue out at him like a five-year-old just as he pulled out of the parking lot.

Easton motioned her ahead of him, as he always did. The growl of Lieutenant Parrish's engine reached her ears as the door swung closed behind them. "Guess he considers himself free from babysitting duty." He nodded as the front desk clerk rounded behind the counter. "Two rooms, please."

"Sorry, I've only got one left, single queen-sized bed. Minimum two-night stay. With the temperatures getting warmer around these parts, we're nearly booked solid for the next month." The clerk held up a single set of keys. "You won't find anything else tonight."

Easton pulled his wallet and tossed a card on the counter. "Book it."

One room. One bed. Pressure built behind her sternum as the clerk gave them directions to a room at the other side of the complex. Easton unlocked the door and kicked it open with his boot. It was exactly as she'd imagined. Dark wood paneling, ugly brown carpeting, a brown bed to match and an air-conditioning unit installed in the only window. She didn't even want to look at the bathroom, but driving back to Battle Mountain tonight was out of the question. Laila Ballard had fallen into the killer's hands, and no matter how many times Captain Morsey threatened to have her arrested, Genevieve was going to find her. Before it was too late.

Easton set his keys and wallet on top of the sixties-style television. "So do you want to be the big spoon or the little spoon?"

HIS ATTEMPT TO lighten the mood struck out.

Genevieve stared at the small room as though it were about to sprout mushrooms from the middle of the floor. Which, in all seriousness, was a possibility. She uncrossed her arms, turning to face him. She lengthened her neck away from her shoulders. "There isn't going to be any spooning because I'm going back to that crime scene."

"Genevieve, you know as well as I do Captain Morsey isn't going to give in. You're still a person of interest in the case. You might not have killed Elisa Johnson yourself, but your house was the stage for her murder." Easton closed the distance between them. "The crime scene unit will be there for hours, and even after they leave, Morsey will have at least two officers stationed for scene security. You're not getting in there on your own."

"I'm not going to be on my own. I have you." She moved around him, cracking the door to peer outside. "Looks like Lieutenant Parrish is gone for now. Hopefully that means he returned to the scene. We can wait a couple of hours. They should be done searching the house by then."

"Oh, well, at least that's cleared up." Easton collapsed onto the edge of the bed. The downpour intensified in the seconds he watched her at the door. "We'll be breaking at least half a dozen laws if we cross that police tape. The district attorney I saw in all those interviews wouldn't even jaywalk let alone disobey a direct order from the police."

She remained poised at the door. "It's not my job I'm worried about."

"I know why you're doing this, Genevieve." The mattress shifted under him as he shoved to his feet. "You feel responsible for what's happened, for Elisa Johnson and for Laila, but putting your career at risk won't get us any closer to finding out who killed those women."

Seconds distorted into minutes the longer she didn't answer. The glow from the sconce outside the room cast angled shadows across her face. But the light, hell, the light highlighted the pain in her expression. Genevieve closed the door. "Do you know why I became a district attorney?"

"No." He shook his head.

"It wasn't to put the bad guys behind bars. I wasn't interested in name recognition or prestige or anything else that comes with this job. None of that matters to me." She set her thumbnail between her teeth and bit down. It was an old habit she hadn't been able to quit long before she'd left Battle Mountain, and he was instantly reminded of the woman he'd fallen in love with all those years ago. "I paid my way through law school and worked my way into Alamosa's good graces to give victims a voice, to make sure their loved ones and families got the justice they deserved. The police, Captain Morsey, they haven't considered the possibility Corey Singleton didn't commit all four of the original murders. Because of me. I saw the connection between Kayleigh Winters's murder and the first three deaths, and I created a narrative that made sense. I made a mistake, and I'm not going to let anyone else die because of it."

Damn. Putting aside the anger—the betrayal—he'd clung to since her arrival at his front doorstep, he couldn't deny his admiration right then. Goose bumps trailed up his arms as he crossed the room. One step. Two. The shag carpet threatened to trip him up along the way, but there was nothing that would stop him from getting to her. "We won't be able to take my truck. Captain Morsey most likely ran the plates to keep tabs on our movements, and the engine is loud as hell. Whichever officers he left as perimeter security will hear us coming from a mile away."

"My car is still parked in my garage a few blocks from here. The scene is a few days old. There shouldn't be any uniformed officers assigned security since the crime scene unit has already been through the house." Surprise infiltrated the soothing notes in her voice. "You're really willing to help me?"

"Yeah, I'm going to help you." As much as he hated the idea of pushing the limits between Alamosa PD and his department, it might be the only way to bring Laila Ballard home before the killer finished the job he'd started with her ear. He skimmed his hands down Genevieve's bare arms and hooked his fingers under her wrists. "That's what partners are for."

"You're not just saying that because you're afraid I'd get myself arrested and rat you out?" she asked.

"That might have been a small part of my decision." He pinched his index finger and thumb together, raising his hand between them. "But a tiny part."

Genevieve used him for balance and rose on her toes. She pressed her mouth to his then lowered back down and set her forehead against his chest. "Thank you. For everything. I wouldn't have gotten this far if it weren't for you."

"I'll start thinking of ways you can pay me back." He kissed the crown of her head. "Until then, we should get some rest and order something in. You're dead on your feet. You look like you're about to fall over."

"Here I thought you might chalk it up to your charming good looks," she said.

"You think I'm charming?" Easton forced himself to release her.

"Don't push it." Her gut-wrenching smile nearly knocked him over as she stared up at him.

Within a few minutes, they'd ordered an unhealthy amount of Chinese food to last them at least three days before trying to distract themselves with something on the out-of-date television. It wasn't long before Genevieve was entering her garage door code into the keypad, and they'd parked a few houses down and across the street from Laila Ballard's home.

The rain had yet to let up, and the wipers worked overtime to keep the windshield clear. Two officers, just as Easton had predicted stood outside the house at the front door. From the look of things, the crime scene unit had cleared out. Captain Morsey had most likely warned his officers not to let the DA or him near the scene, but there was a chance his stunt having them followed to the motel eased his suspicions. Easton shouldered out the passenger side door of her too-small sedan. "I'll meet you at the back."

"Be careful." Genevieve cut the engine, fisted her keys and hit the sidewalk. In a matter of seconds, she disappeared into the shadows alongside the neighbor's side yard to cut through another property.

They'd been over the plan a dozen times. Get in. Get out. No mistakes.

Easton's boots echoed off the cracked sidewalk as he approached Laila Ballard's home and the crime scene tape strung up to keep nosey reserve officers out. He waved to the two officers descending the steps. He didn't recognize either of them from earlier. Perhaps their luck would hold. He flashed his Battle Mountain PD badge. "Evening, fellas. Captain Morsey thought I might be able to lend a hand to the investigation of the missing woman who lives here. I'm going to need to take a look at the scene."

"We weren't notified anyone outside of the department would be consulting on this case." The nearest officer set his hand against Easton's chest. "We're going to have to call the captain."

Easton studied the hand on his chest and recalled all the different bones he could break in one move, but he wasn't here to start a war between their departments. All he had to do was get inside. "You go ahead and do that. You call him after he's been at this scene almost all day, after he's probably just sat down for dinner with his wife and turned on his favorite after-shift show. Let's see how that plays out for you."

Hesitation lined the officer's eyes as he slid his gaze to his partner. "Captain hates it when we interrupt his *Jeopardy* reruns."

"Yeah, all right." The second officer waved him past. "Make it quick though, will you? Our shift change is in twenty minutes."

"I'll do my best. Thank you, boys." Easton climbed the front steps of the rambler-style home. At the door, he pulled two sets of protective booties from the cardboard box and wrapped one over his boots. Fisting the other, he closed the door behind him. CSU had laid out a specific path for investigators to follow through the house with markers. A bedroom door stood open directly to his right, a small half bath directly after that before the hallway opened into a wide room. The open kitchen had been set off to his left with the living room opposite, and through the laundry room past that, he spotted a sliding glass door leading to the back patio.

The home wasn't large by any standard, but enough for the single mother Genevieve had described. Family photos decorated the mantel in the living room, staring him down, as he picked up the pace. Unlocking the sliding glass door, Easton whistled two short bursts into the darkness.

No answer. No sign of movement.

He waited another minute. "Genevieve."

Still nothing.

The hairs at the back of his neck stood on end as he stepped out onto the back patio. Rain pattered off the tall oaks lining the back of the property. Had she not been able to get into the backyard? They'd known there was a slim chance of the officers out front not recognizing her from the amount of face-to-face time she'd spent with the department and as a person of interest in the Elisa Johnson case. Going around through the back had been their only option. But now... "Genevieve?"

She should've been here by now. He walked to the north side of the house, but only met a row of bare rose bushes and thorns. It was too dark to see if there were any fresh tracks through the well-manicured grass. Genevieve most likely would've come over the neighbor's wood fence, and he put one foot in front of the other until he reached the end.

He kicked something solid. A metallic clink filtered through the constant tick of rain. A sprinkler head? No. He toed the object with his boot. Sprinkler heads didn't move unless they'd been decapitated by the lawnmower. Crouching low, Easton ran his hand through the grass. His fingers hit solid metal, and he clenched the object in his palm.

A set of keys.

The light from the back patio highlighted the vehicle key fob. Same manufacturer as Genevieve's. He hit the red panic button. An alarm blared from where they'd parked her car down the block, and it was then he knew.

She was gone.

Chapter Eight

"If you scream, I'll kill you, then I'll kill him."
Movement—footsteps?—registered a few feet away.
Twigs snapped under a heavy weight from nearby.

Genevieve dragged her chin away from her chest,
but an unfamiliar heaviness forced her to overcorrect, and her head fell back. Pain ricocheted through
her skull as rough bark scraped against her scalp.
A tree. Damp earth soaked into her slacks, but she
couldn't see much farther than maybe a foot to tell
where she was. Cold spits of rain pelted her face,
the soft rhythm bouncing off foliage and leaves.
"Where...where am I?"

She was...supposed to meet Easton at the back of
Laila Ballard's house. She'd gone through the side
yard of one of the neighbor's properties, cutting in
front of the tree line, and then... She couldn't remember. Why couldn't she remember? A shiver chased
up her arms and down her spine. April had fooled

them all, promising spring when there was nothing but bone-deep coldness in the dark.

"Someplace Officer Ford will never find you." Another shift of movement, closer than before. A ski mask and a white ring of eyes materialized to her left, and Genevieve pressed her heels into the ground to gain some semblance of distance. In vain. He kept his voice low, almost whispery. "Don't worry, I'm not going to hurt you, Genevieve. At least, not yet. You and I have a lot to talk about first."

Fractures of memory arced to the front of her mind. The neighbor's backyard, the feeling of being watched. The shadow that hadn't really been a shadow at all. She'd tried to scream, but he'd put an end to that before any sound had the chance to leave her mouth.

"You were waiting for me." It was the only possibility that made sense. But how would he have known she'd return to the crime scene? Genevieve blinked to clear the last of the dizziness. Had he followed her and Easton, or… "The ear. You sent it to me at the motel. You followed me from Alamosa to Battle Mountain. You knew I wouldn't be able to get involved in the case, but I would still try to find out who it came from. You used Laila Ballard to lure me here."

And she'd fallen straight into his trap.

"I have to tell you, I'm quite impressed you were

able to discern who the ear belongs to, especially considering how careful I was not to leave any identifying markers." His voice—familiar and strange at the same time—grated against her nerves. "But if you'd just been a little faster, I wouldn't have needed to use her to motivate you at all."

"Laila." She tried to move her wrists from her lower back, but only met the sharp sting of plastic biting into her skin. Zip ties? He must've secured her wrists and ankles while she'd been unconscious. There was no give between the plastic and her skin. A tendril of fear combined with memories from the break-in at her home, and the air crushed from her lungs. Had he brought her here to show her Laila's body? Would her senses catch up with the darkness enough to outline her friend's remains nearby? Nausea churned hard and fast. "What did you do with her?"

"We'll get to that," he said. "First, I need to know what else you and Officer Ford have discovered over the course of this investigation."

Officer Ford. He knew. He knew about Easton. He hadn't just studied her. He'd wanted her to know how far his reach extended, but she wouldn't let him use the Ford family for whatever endgame he had in mind. Not what Dr. Miles had uncovered. Not the interviews Weston Ford conducted. And not the leads Easton had pulled from the victim files.

"Nothing." Genevieve pressed her head back into the tree. The pain intensified enough to keep her in the moment, to counteract whatever he'd done to her to knock her out. Blunt force trauma? A sedative? The memories were out of reach. She rolled her head from side to side. "I swear."

"You're lying to me, Genevieve. Do it again, and I'll have no use for you. You'll end up exactly as the others. Only I'll make sure your broken toy soldier is there when I screw the eyelets into your joints." The low slide of metal reached her ears a split second before cool steel pressed against her neck. Not the sharpness of a blade as before. Something duller. Stronger. Thicker with a bite. The answer settled at the back of her throat. A drill bit. "I know Captain Morsey banned you from the investigation, but you didn't get to be a district attorney by giving up. Tell me about the 9-1-1 call made by Maria Gutierrez, the one you manipulated the dispatcher into sharing with you."

Every cell in her body caught fire. "How—"

"A true artist never reveals his secrets," he said.

"That's what you think you are? An artist?" This was nothing but a game to him, a way to stay close to the investigation, to stay ahead of police. No. She wasn't going to give him anything. She leaned away from the tree to gauge if he'd tied her to it. The drill bit nicked the side of her neck, but she didn't stop.

Her knuckles grazed against soil and dead leaves. If she could break the zip ties, she'd have the chance to escape. She had to keep him talking. Distracted. "You murder innocent women. You string them up as though they're nothing but dolls, and I'm not telling you anything."

"That's too bad." Puffs of crystalized exhales escaped through the lower half of his ski mask. No identifying features. Nothing to tell her who'd terrorized and killed four women over the course of a year, one of which he'd staged in her own home. "I was hoping you'd last longer than the others. I thought you were different. You were supposed to be the strongest, but you're just like them, aren't you? Weak. Self-righteous. Emotionally compromised."

Genevieve set her jaw. She strained against the outer edge of the zip ties and increased the pressure between her wrists. "I tend to get emotional when someone kills the people I care about."

"You know, that's why I've always liked you. Even under the threat of physical harm, you don't deviate from your beliefs. We're the same in that regard." A low laugh rumbled into the small space between them. "But if you're not going to tell me what I want to know, I have to find someone who will, and you will be the reason they suffer. You see, just as you don't know who you are without your work, I can't live without mine. But to keep my edge, I have to make the game more challenging. So every woman who dies from here on out will be because of you. They will suffer more because you failed to stop me. Are you sure you're willing to live with that, Genevieve?"

"Go to hell." Genevieve hauled both feet into her chest and kicked out hard. Her heels rocketed into her attacker, and a vicious growl cut through the white noise of rain. She pushed to her feet as fast as she could, unbalanced, but still breathing. She dropped into a squat and severed the ties around her ankles. She didn't have time to claw through the zip ties at her wrists. She had to run. Shadows closed around her. Exertion burned down the backs of her thighs as she sprinted across uneven ground, but she wouldn't stop. She didn't know where she'd been held, where she was going. It didn't matter. "Help me!"

Her scream tore up the back of her throat, but she pushed herself harder. Cold settled at the bottom of her lungs. Rocks and fallen branches threatened to trip her up. She had to keep going. She had to find Easton. The killer couldn't have taken her far during the few short minutes she'd been unconscious, which meant they were most likely still in Laila Ballard's neighborhood. "Help!"

Lightning arced across the sky and highlighted a section of thinning trees up ahead. A way out. Swinging her bound hands back and forth in front of her, Genevieve breathed a sigh of relief. She was almost there. She could see something on the other side of the tree line.

The cover of trees vanished as she burst through a growth of bushes lining the property, and she froze. No. Her breath left her in a rush. She didn't understand. Disbelief curdled in her stomach. It wasn't possible. She shook her head to rewind the past few minutes, but there was no denying the truth. They weren't in Laila Ballard's neighborhood anymore. He'd dragged her away from Alamosa altogether.

The Great Sand Dunes National Park stretched for miles out in front of her. Wet sand built up along the bottom of her shoes. Fourteen-thousand-foot peaks demanded attention along the Sangre de Cristo mountain range, the enormity of her situation draining the blood from her face. "Run."

The single word nearly ripped from her chest as she struggled through the quicksand terrain. Warm liquid combined with numbing rain between her wrists. Blood. She couldn't stop. No matter how much it hurt. Her breath sawed in and out of her chest as she dug her boots into the side of the nearest peak. If she could get to the other side, out of sight, there was a chance the killer wouldn't follow. Question was: Was she worth the trouble? The sick feeling in her gut intensified as she considered the answer.

A grittiness stung her face and neck as she

rounded the first peak. Genevieve tried to block the onslaught with her bound hands, but it wasn't enough. A little farther. She could already make out the outline of the next peak. She might have a chance if she picked up the pace.

A wall of muscle slammed into her from behind.

She pitched forward and hit the ground. Sand filled her mouth and nose as she struggled to unpin her wrists from beneath her. Her lungs spasmed for oxygen, but the weight on her back refused to let up. Pain seared across her scalp as her attacker pulled her head back by her hair, exposing her throat from chin to her collar.

"Did you think I'd let you get away so easily?" He flipped her onto her back and grasped her throat. Pulling her closer, the killer leveled his crazed gaze with hers as she struggled for oxygen. He threw her back into the sand, grabbed hold of her ankles and dragged her back toward the trees. "I made you the woman you are, Genevieve. You don't get to walk away from me."

HE'D SEARCHED THE entire area.

The treads he'd matched to the bottom of Genevieve's boots had ended at the neighbor's back property line. There was no sign of her, but another set of prints—deeper, wider and longer than the district attorney's—had taken her place.

Someone had been out here. Someone had taken her, and Easton couldn't think of anyone else other than the killer who'd lured them here in the first place. None of the other victims had been dismembered, making Laila Ballard special. The killer had studied Genevieve well enough to know she wouldn't stop until they had an identification, and when she realized her friend had become a victim, he'd known she'd come running. The entire scene had become a trap, but Easton hadn't seen it in time.

He sped around to the front of the house and caught sight of the two officers assigned to secure the scene. "Call your captain. We've got a problem." He explained as much of the situation Alamosa PD needed to know then unpocketed his phone. He scrolled through the screen and hit the contact he needed. The line connected almost instantly, but he wouldn't waste time with politeness. "Genevieve's been taken. Ten to fifteen minutes ago, from Laila Ballard's home. Alamosa PD is on alert, but I need you here."

"I'm leaving now." The scrape of metal on wood pierced through the line as Weston set into action. "Listen to me, no matter what happens, remember he wants something from her. He won't kill her unless he has to, and we don't want to force his hand. Where would he take her?"

Easton scrubbed a hand down his face as the all

too familiar sense of helplessness bubbled to the surface. Rain cascaded in lines along his neck. He stared out into the neighborhood. Pressure built behind his sternum as he ran through his limited knowledge of the area. "I don't know. All of his kills have been in Alamosa. This is his hunting grounds, but I'm in unfamiliar territory."

"It wouldn't be the first time, Easton. Think. He'll have to take her somewhere private, isolated enough to give him the upper hand. Somewhere you'd never think to look for her. This killer is one of the rare types that wants to get caught, but he's not going to go down without a fight. He'll do whatever it takes to win." The distant rumbling of a truck engine filtered through the panic setting up residence in Easton's mind. Weston was already on his way, but it would take at least three hours for his brother to get here. Genevieve didn't have that kind of time. "Chloe's been through all of the autopsy reports for the victims. She didn't find anything out of the ordinary, but there's a chance we missed something. I'll have her run through them again."

"Guys like this don't kill where they sleep. He went out of his way to contain the forensics inside the victims' homes, including Genevieve's. He's not going to take the risk of evidence leading back to him. He's too careful for that." Damn it. They had nothing. Easton braced his weight against the vinyl fence of the wraparound porch as a single truth penetrated through the haze of loss. He'd battled like hell to deny it, but the past forty-eight hours had obliterated his control when it came to that woman. "I can't lose her again, Weston."

"You won't," his brother said. "I'll be there as soon as I can. Until then, I'll call you if Chloe comes up with anything."

"Thanks." Easton ended the call.

"Captain isn't answering." The first officer stepped into his peripheral vision. "We've tried half a dozen times, but there's no response from him or Lieutenant Parrish."

Parrish. The officer who'd escorted him and Genevieve back to the hotel. The edgy smile Lieutenant Parrish had given Easton when they'd been removed from the scene had seared clearly into his memory. They'd been face-to-face with the officer for less than two minutes, but the man had left a hell of an impression. Without Captain Morsey or his right hand answering their phones, Easton was on his own. "You two come with me."

"With all due respect, Officer Ford, this isn't Battle Mountain," the second officer said. "Until Captain Morsey or Lieutenant Parrish tell us otherwise, we've been ordered to stay here to secure this scene."

He didn't have time for this. "Listen to me, the woman who lives here has been taken by a killer. He cut off her ear and sent it to the district attorney to lure her to this scene. Now, DA Alexander is missing, and I have reason to believe that same killer is behind her abduction. I'm not asking for permission. I'm telling you she's in trouble, and it's your duty to help me find her."

His heart threatened to beat straight out of his chest as both officers glanced to one another. "Yes, sir. Tell us what you need."

"Lieutenant Parrish. What do you know about him?" he asked. "Where does he live?"

"You're not suggesting the lieutenant is behind this." A scoff escaped the first officer's mouth.

"I don't know, but Genevieve Alexander and Laila Ballard are running out of time." Knowledge of forensics, seemingly familiar with the Alamosa PD playbook, constantly one step ahead—a law enforcement officer's involvement made sense. If the killer was involved in the case, he could lead the investigation any direction he wanted, but that didn't get them anywhere close to a location the bastard might be hiding two innocent women. As for Lieutenant Parrish, there was something in the officer's expression earlier that Easton couldn't get out of his mind. He thought back over what Weston had said. The killer would need somewhere isolated, private enough to keep uninvited guests from interrupting his playtime with his victims. "Does Parrish have experience with tools or own any properties outside of town?"

"Actually, yeah," the second officer said. "Parrish runs a construction company on his off hours. His cabin is just outside of the national park, along the southern end of the dunes."

Easton's gut twisted. A cabin was perfect. Out of the way, quiet. "Take me there."

Both officers raced for their patrol vehicle while Easton fisted the keys he'd found in the backyard and collapsed behind the wheel of Genevieve's sedan. Headlights cut through the darkness as he fell in behind Alamosa PD. They wound through the neighborhood then shot up the main streets of the growing city before the valley stretched out in front of him.

The low ringing vibrated in his ears, and he blinked to fight off the oncoming sensory overload, but it was too late. He'd lost control. The barrenness of the landscape transformed in front of him, night turning to day, temperatures rising in the too-small cab of the car. His pulse rocketed into his throat as the first of the flashbacks hit hard and fast. An echo of laughter replaced the constant tick of rain, and his mind urged him to relax. It was just a simple supply run. Sweat built in his hairline under his helmet as he scanned the faces of his unit. The thud of Watowski's weight against the side of the truck pulled Easton's attention from the road.

By the time he turned back, it'd been too late.

The explosion came out of nowhere.

Shouts replaced laughter. The entire vehicle was engulfed in flames and heat and pain. Until there was nothing but smoke and screams.

His vision wavered. Red and blue patrol lights distorted in his vision ahead. He hadn't been able to help them—any of them—but he wouldn't fail Genevieve. He'd find her in time. He'd keep her alive and bring down the killer terrorizing women in Alamosa.

Easton released the breath he hadn't realized he'd been holding. The memories were still there. Waiting. But, stronger than the past, was the woman he'd planned to marry. The windshield wipers worked overtime. High, smooth peaks of sand took shape outside the driver's side window as thick trees blacked out the Sangre de Cristo Mountains to his right. The tendons in his hands ached from his grip on the steering wheel, and he forced himself to focus. "Come on. Where are you, you bastard?"

The patrol vehicle less than twenty feet ahead skidded to a stop in the middle of the road. Dim lighting outlined a small angular cabin with a raised front porch, red-painted roof and what looked like a new set of handrails leading up the ten steps to the main door. Easton slammed on the brakes before the car's front grill met the back of the patrol vehicle's bumper and shoved the vehicle into Park. He hit the frozen ground still covered with patches of ice and unspoiled snow. She was here. He could feel it. He pointed to the two officers spilling out of their car. "Keep trying to get a hold of Captain Morsey!"

He hurried up the steep steps, the stairs shaking under his weight. Hauling his heel into the wood beside the untarnished dead bolt, Easton kicked open the front door. He scanned the small space, taking in the swell of cold and emptiness. No. Damn it, she had to be here. He searched the main living room, ran his hands over the stones of the fireplace and scoured for clues through the only bedroom in the back. Empty. Panic gripped him by the throat. "Where the hell are you?"

He stepped out onto the front porch. His exhales crystalized in front of his mouth. Temperatures had dipped below freezing. He squeezed his hand around the new guardrail. He'd been wrong. He'd taken the evidence and warped it to fit his own theory. Hell, he wasn't any better than the killer, only this mistake would cost Genevieve and Laila Ballard their lives.

Easton memorized a fresh pattern carved into the ground. Narrowing his gaze, he jogged down the stairs. He crouched a few feet from the corner of the cabin and traced a long length of tire tracks. Someone had been out here recently. Within the past few hours. His instincts pushed him to his feet. "I need a flashlight."

One of the officers handed him their light. "We're still trying to get a hold of the captain. No answer from Lieutenant Parrish either."

Because the lieutenant was out here.

Easton didn't have proof. Nothing to connect Parrish to any of the murders. Nothing but a feeling. It would have to be enough. Easton followed the length of the tire treads, past the property line. Deeper. The rain had made a mess of everything and drew sand from the edge of the dunes into the woods. He swept the beam up ahead and landed on the distinct outline in the distance. He slowed. Denial lodged in his throat. "Genevieve?"

No answer. No movement.

Easton scanned the surrounding trees as he closed in on her. Her feet swayed above the ground. No. No, no, no, no. He lost his hold on the flashlight and sprinted through mud and loose rock. Circling his arm around her waist, he hoisted her higher to relieve the tension of the fishing line round her neck.

Her gasp filled the clearing.

Chapter Nine

"Are you experiencing any discomfort, Ms. Alexander?" The doctor pulled the curtain, cutting off Genevieve's view of the rest of the hospital. The screen of her tablet reflected a bright glare from overhead flourescent lights as the attending took a seat on the stool. She set the tablet onto the table beside the bed. "May I?"

Genevieve nodded. "I was…strung up from a tree with fishing line and left to die." Rawness prickled along the edges of her throat. It hurt to swallow, to talk, to move her head, but every streak of pain reminded her she was still alive. Somehow. "Yes, I'm experiencing discomfort."

"From what I've been able to tell from your scans, your jugular veins were compressed for at least a full minute, but the damage didn't extend to the carotid arteries." The physician kept her touch light as she prodded Genevieve's throat. "Seems Officer Ford pulled you down just in time. You're a very lucky woman. Thirty seconds more, and you'd be in a different room altogether."

She didn't remember that part. Easton pulling her down. There was a lot she didn't remember, but her subconscious must've registered he'd been with her in the woods because her only thought had been of him. She traced her thumb along the gauze around her wrists. The lacerations underneath stung, but the ibuprofen the nurses had given her helped. Tears burned in her eyes, and Genevieve quickly swiped them from her face.

"Did that hurt?" Concern lightened the doctor's touch.

She tried to shake her head, reminded of the stiffness in the muscles along her neck and jaw. From what she'd been told, the killer had strung her up in the tree by the neck, but had positioned the zip ties around her wrists to take most of her weight. He hadn't been trying to kill her. At least, not quickly, but how much longer was she supposed to play this game? How much longer until Easton discovered her hanging from her ceiling with steel eyelets screwed into her joints and fishing line taking all of her weight? "No, I just…"

Just, what? Just wanted to go home? Her home had been broken into, turned into a crime scene and violated. Wanted to forget? There was nothing that could erase those terrifying hours from her memory.

Understanding swept across the physician's expression, and she pulled back slightly. "You've been through a trauma. Not just physically. It'll take some time for these bruises to heal, but more importantly... Ms. Alexander, is there anyone you can talk to?"

"Um." No. There wasn't. Laila Ballard had already suffered because of her connection to Genevieve. She wouldn't put anyone else in danger. "I'm fine."

"Okay." Suspicion replaced understanding as the doctor stood, but she knew as well as Genevieve did, if a patient wouldn't accept help, there was nothing she could do. "We'll keep you pain-free with the ibuprofen, but if the soreness gets worse, let me know. I don't think we'll need to keep you longer than tonight, if you're ready to go home. I recommend a liquid diet over the next few days to prevent any tearing. Be sure to stay hydrated and get plenty of rest."

"Thank you. Do you... Could you tell me where Officer Ford is?" she asked.

"I'll have one of the nurses track him down and send him your way." The scrape of the metal rings around the curtain grated against her senses as the attending enclosed her back into the circle of fabric and privacy.

Privacy was a misleading word. Because on the

other side of that thin fabric was the low echo of dispatches from the PA system, squeaky wheels from long-past-their-prime gurneys, orders from physicians, steady footsteps of other nurses and staff. Yet, despite the number of people around her, Genevieve had never felt so alone. She smoothed her thumb over the call button of the remote attached to her bed. Closing her eyes, she tried to ignore the building agony behind her sternum. She could still feel the grittiness of the sand in her hair, smell the wet leaves on her skin. The crime scene unit had taken and bagged her clothes as evidence when she'd been brought in, but she was still living the nightmare with every inhale.

"You look like you could use one of these," a warm, familiar voice said.

Genevieve pried her eyes open when all she wanted to do was sink deeper into the pillows stacked behind her. She couldn't fight the slight tug of her mouth as she took in the mud still streaked across his face. Steam escaped from the small semicircle hole at the top of the large to-go cup he offered and curled between them. She stretched her free hand out, the other tied down with an IV and the blood pressure cuff. "That doesn't smell like coffee."

"Bone broth. Homemade. I keep a couple bottles in my truck for emergencies, and the nurses were nice enough to let me use one of their microwaves."

Easton rolled the stool her doctor had occupied a few minutes ago between his legs and sat down, his own cup in hand. "Figured your throat might be sore for a bit. Considering you might not get to eat something for a while, this was the only thing I could think of that wouldn't make you feel like you were starving to death."

"Thank you." Scents of salt, carrots, celery, chicken and a few spices she didn't recognize filled her lungs. The heat bled into her hands and battled to chase back the cold that seemed to have permanently set up residence in her bones. She managed a sip and was instantly surrendered to the comfort she craved. Genevieve raised the cup. "This is really good. I take it your family knows I'm back in town."

Easton took a swig from his own serving. "I had Weston ready to run you off the property with his shotgun if I gave the signal, but my mother doesn't know you're here yet."

"The signal?" It hurt to laugh, but the simple act relaxed the tendons down the back of her neck and between her shoulder blades. "Let me guess. Smoke signals from the chimney."

"Better. A secret Ford family whistle." He collected her cup from her and set it on the table beside the bed. "Every time we went out hunting when Weston and I were growing up, we would let each other know where we were on the property with this whistle. Made it so we were less likely to shoot each other."

She smoothed her palms over the invisible creases in the sheets. "I always admired your family, how happy you all were. I remember one time knocking on your family cabin front door to see you after school, but no one inside heard me because you were all laughing too hard. I stood there waiting for a few minutes until the laughter died down so I could knock again. My hands were frozen by the time I got the chance."

"Those were the good old days." Easton stared down at his cup, tracing the edge of the lid with the side of his knuckle. "Before...everything went to hell. Before the military sent me home and Weston became the police chief. Before dad died." He took another swig of his broth, but Genevieve had the feeling the action had more to do with distraction than any need for a drink.

"I heard about your dad through the grapevine. I'm sorry," she said.

"He died doing exactly what he'd taught us to do for others. Fight for and defend them until our last breath. The man who killed him was trying to get to Chloe, and Dad wasn't going to have that." Easton cleared his throat. "He's the one who got Weston through losing his wife a few years ago, managed to convince him to watch over this town when Chief

Frasier couldn't do the job anymore to work through the grief. James Ford was a great man, I'll give you that. No matter how many times I slammed the door in his face those first few months I was home, he'd always come back. He'd hand me a shovel and tell me the land wasn't going to work itself, and that I had a lot of work ahead of me."

"You turned out all right." She'd missed this. Them just talking as though they'd picked up right where they'd left off all those years ago.

"Yeah." A lightness seemed to brighten the sea-blue color of his eyes for a moment. Something she hadn't seen since she'd showed her face in Battle Mountain. "Guess I did."

A thrill of being the center of this man's world raised goose bumps along her arms, and Genevieve ducked her chin to her chest. Falling back into old routines and patterns, falling for him and this town all over again, the familiarity and warmth, would only lead to one place: invisibility. She'd worked too hard to make an identity for herself, to prove she was more than that teenaged girl who knew nothing about the world or the people in it. She wasn't going to throw it all away now. She couldn't. She cleared her throat, but the pain was too much to do any good. "Was the crime scene unit able to find something from Laila Ballard's house that could lead them to her?"

Easton leaned back on the stool. Moment over. "Yeah. They recovered a set of footprints at the back of the property where yours disappeared, but the rain had washed a lot of the ridges away. From what Alamosa PD can tell, they're a match for a set recovered at the scene of your home. They managed to cast a partial print and compared it to those left near Lieutenant Parrish's cabin near the dunes where we found you. They were a perfect match. Captain Morsey was all too willing to give me and Weston access once the match was made. Turns out, Parrish is the one who responded to Maria Gutierrez's 9-1-1 call two weeks before she turned up dead in her home. He was the closest. The current theory is he suspected she was on to him and wanted to keep an eye on her. We're in the process of getting a search warrant for Parrish's main residence and access to his phone records and financials. With any luck, we'll find something there that will lead us to Laila."

Lieutenant Parrish. The officer who'd escorted them to the motel? "You think he might be the killer."

"He almost killed you, Genevieve. He would have if I hadn't gotten to you in time. The son of a bitch hung you from a tree with fishing line around your throat, but from what your doctor said, he ensured most of your weight was in your wrists. He wanted me to find you like that. He wanted me to know he could take you from me," he said. "This is nothing but a sick game he thinks he can win, but I won't let him. Okay? I give you my word, I won't stop until he's in cuffs or in the ground. So is there anything you remember that will help me find him?"

"He said…" Defiance coiled low in her belly. "He made me who I am."

EASTON CLEARED THE CABIN.

With Lieutenant Parrish still in the wind, he couldn't take any chances. Morsey's right-hand man had disconnected the GPS on his cruiser and turned off his phone, and the search of his home revealed he'd left his credit cards behind. They'd lost him.

CSU hadn't been able to come up with anything from the latest scene. Every surface capable of giving them a fingerprint had been wiped down. No DNA or fibers recovered from the tree Genevieve had been hung from or from the zip ties used to secure her wrists. The killer was covering his tracks, making it impossible for them to get a positive ID, and staying one step ahead. Alamosa's forensics unit had tried running the partial recovered from the package with Laila Ballard's ear inside a second time, but there still wasn't enough to match anyone in the system.

"Clear." He crossed back to the front door and reached for Genevieve to bring her inside. "I'll get a fire going. We'll have you warmed up and comfortable in no time." He tossed in a few logs from the basket beside the stone fireplace and set about feeding the kindling to start. Within a few minutes, heat sped through him and the rest of the cabin.

"Guess you lost out on your deposit for the motel room, huh?" Scanning the space, she looked as though she were stepping into it for the very first time. Cautious. Alert. Strung tight. She hadn't said a word since her discharge from the hospital or during the three-hour drive back to Battle Mountain. Exhaustion carved deep hollows into her cheeks, and right then, Easton wanted nothing more than to take her pain away. Mentally and physically. "You know you don't have to stay with me."

"The last time I left you alone, a killer dragged you out into the middle of the national park and strung you from a tree." He wrenched open the linen closet door and tugged a stack of pillows and blankets down from the top shelf. Tossing them onto the couch, he spread them out as any man who'd become accustomed to sleeping on the ground using a rock as a pillow would. "I'm not going anywhere."

He could protect her here. This was his territory. His gut said the killer would try for her again, but next time, Easton would be there. He would be ready.

Long fingers curled around his forearm, forcing him to slow down. "It wasn't your fault. The killer... He changed his MO. We had no reason to believe he'd use another victim to lure me to that scene, and blaming yourself for something you can't control will only eat at you until there's nothing left."

He memorized the ridges of her knuckles, the scrapes across the backs of her hands. He released his grip on the blankets and turned to face her. Sliding his hand beneath hers, he traced the edge of her bandaged wrists with his thumb. "I should've been there."

"You were," she said.

Confusion cut through him. "What do you—"

"I wasn't scared." Confidence registered in her voice, and the unsettled tremors he'd noted in her fingers a couple days ago had since vanished. "When he had me, when he tried to tell me every woman he'd kill in the future would suffer because of me, the only thing I could think of was you. You were with me. I knew you'd realize I'd been taken. I knew you wouldn't stop until you found me. I…knew you'd be there when I needed you the most. At that point, there was nothing he could say or do to hurt me."

He traced the patterns of fresh scabs and bruises left by the fishing line across her neck with the tips of his fingers, and she closed her eyes. As though she trusted him. Dark splotches marred her perfect skin, but it was the thin laceration across her throat that would scar, that would announce to the world what she'd survived. "Genevieve, I'm not who you think I am. I'm not some knight in shining armor—"

"No, you're not." Genevieve secured her hands under his ears and forced him to confront her head on. "You're stronger. You fight for others harder than you fight for yourself, and you'll go down with the ship to save the relationships you've managed to hold on to. Just as you did with us, like you did with your unit and your brother when he and Chloe were in danger a few months ago. You're loyal and committed to everyone who comes into your life, no matter how strained the connection. You see that dedication as a weakness and a vulnerability, something your enemies can target because your brain is still trying to process all that trauma. But the truth is, it makes you one of the most admirable men I've ever met. Despite what you think, I know you. Inside and out, and I'm not saying any of this because if it weren't for you, I wouldn't be standing here." Her voice softened as she lowered her hands to her sides. "Although, that does have a small part to do with it."

Process trauma. Is that what his brain was trying to do? Make sense of what'd happened after all this time? Army shrinks had tried to help. His dad had tried to push him to open up. Weston did everything he could to force him back into the real world, but none of them were Genevieve. None of them had ever looked at him as anything more than a broken soldier, and it was only then he realized he loved her for it. After all these years, all the anger, he still loved her. Hell. Easton skimmed his hand down the back of her arm.

"When I was following those two Alamosa PD officers out to the dunes, I was back in that moment. In Afghanistan. Right before everything went to hell." He braced for the ringing in his ears, the first sign of another episode about to tear him apart. Only it never came. "We were assigned to make a simple supply run. Watowski had made a rotten joke and Ripper slugged him for it. She didn't appreciate the punch line, and she was a hell of a lot stronger than she looked. A few of the other guys were laughing. Watowski hit the side of the truck, and I turned around. Everyone was smiling, including me. We'd created a bubble of normalcy inside the terror we dealt with on a daily basis. In that moment, we were happy."

He'd never told anyone the details. Definitely not anyone in his family, but the weight of her attention, the feel of her skin against his, somehow settled the raging horror he'd lived with the past year. "After we hit the IED, I didn't know which way was up. I think I knew what'd happened. I remember I pulled every single one of them from the truck, but at the time it was like watching someone else do it from afar. I didn't realize a piece of shrapnel had penetrated my helmet until a sergeant from one of the other trucks pulled me away. I wanted to help them, but it was too late." The truth reverberated through him. "I didn't want to be too late for you, too."

"You weren't." Genevieve rose onto her toes and wrapped her arms around his neck. Her heart thumped hard against his chest. Strong, reliable. She buried her mouth between his neck and shoulder and pressed her mouth to his skin. Then again. Trailing her lips up the length of his neck, she craned her head back and skimmed her teeth along his jaw. "I told you. I'm here. However you need me. I'm here."

An explosion of desire lightninged through him, and Easton reached back to grip her hands in each of his. "Genevieve, don't." He shook his head, every nerve ending he owned on fire. Tension constricted the muscles down his spine. "Don't give me hope."

"Maybe I'm the one who needs hope tonight." Her mouth met his in a battle for dominance. Mint burst across his tongue as she penetrated the seam of his lips. Angling her head, she opened wider, surrendering.

Easton maneuvered her backward until she hit the frame of the couch. Heat that had nothing to do with the roaring fire worked under his collar. Her fingers speared through his hair, nails scratching against his scalp. Hiking her thighs around his hips, he balanced her with the help of the couch then hauled her into him. A soft moan escaped her control and shot a wave of desire into overdrive.

This. This was what he'd missed about her. This connection. The invisible understanding they'd always shared. He'd felt it that first time he'd laid eyes on her in the high school cafeteria, and he felt it now. Maneuvering her around to the front of the couch, Easton settled her onto the pillows and blankets he'd intended to use as a makeshift bed. She'd always known how to talk to him, to handle him, when to back off and when to push him over the edge. It was a feat few had accomplished, and he admired the hell out of her for it.

Because she was right.

She did know him, inside and out, and he knew her. Every curve, every scar, every button to press and how far to push her before she pushed back. She was everything he remembered and everything he didn't want to live without. Contradictory to the danger surrounding her, she'd continually held her head high and given one of the most vicious killers he'd known the middle finger, and damn, if that wasn't the sexiest thing he'd ever seen.

"Tonight, you deserve not to have to hold yourself together. Tonight, you can let the cracks in that legendary armor show. I'll take care of you, Genevieve. I promise." He settled his weight over her and tucked a strand of hair behind her ear. "Tell me what you need."

Flames reflected in her gaze. She hesitated in the

process of unbuttoning his shirt. Attention on him, Genevieve let her guard slip away. The district attorney he'd studied on TV over the years vanished, leaving the sensitive, isolated woman underneath. Pain reflected in her expression, and in that moment, his purpose, the one his father had been trying to get him to see long before now, became clear.

Everything he'd gone through—Genevieve leaving, the IED, the PTSD, losing his father two months ago—it'd led him right to this moment. It'd made him strong enough to help her and others still lost in that drowning darkness they couldn't escape. He had. Because of her.

She smoothed her thumb under his eye, and he leaned into her hand. "Make me forget. Please. Make me forget."

Chapter Ten

Heat chased across her skin.

Genevieve rolled deeper into the mountain of blankets they'd escaped under last night. A scraping sound reached her ears. Pressing her eyes together harder, she tried to fall back into the sweet release of unconsciousness, but the smell of coffee and eggs triggered hunger. Coffee, eggs and…something sweet. She stretched her toes to the bottom of the makeshift bed. Small muscles she'd forgotten existed protested at the slightest strain, and the flood of pleasure, whispers and a sense of safety charged forward.

She'd had boyfriends over the years. Nothing serious, but enough to satisfy her cravings. But last night, with Easton… She'd forgotten how reactive she could be under his touch. Genevieve peeled her eyes open. A couple more logs had been added to the fire. She brushed her hair back away from her face, all too aware of the feel of the blankets over her bare skin. She turned onto her stomach to watch him in the kitchen. She wedged her knuckles under her chin, captivated, but was quickly reminded of the soreness around her throat.

He kept his back to her, the muscles rippling and releasing across his shoulders as he worked. Larger than life. He'd adorned his jeans with a black apron tied at the back of his neck and around his lean hips. He didn't have to turn around for her to know the front read "Meat is murder! Tasty, tasty murder." The apron had been on their wedding registry, and his father had agreed with the slogan enough to buy it for them.

"I didn't realize you'd kept that." She secured the closest blanket under her arms and held on to the edges as she stood. Cold darted up her bare feet as she made her way into the kitchen. She tucked the corner of the blanket between her breasts, reached for a mug from the cabinet to his left and poured herself a cup of coffee. Leaning her hip against the counter, she faced him. "The apron. It looks good on you."

His laugh tendrilled through her and raised her awareness into heightened territory. His hair had taken on a life of its own through the night, revitalizing that boyhood charm she'd fallen for. "Figure as long as I look good, I could get away with cooking a pot of air, and no one would notice."

"I certainly wouldn't." Mug in one hand, she slid her hand along his lower back and hiked onto her toes. She pressed her mouth to his, a fraction of the desire she'd felt last night blistering her lips. She nearly dropped the mug as Easton left whatever concoction he was cooking in the pan and pulled her hips in line with his. Her mouth parted under his deepening assault. She dug the tips of her fingers into his spine as he memorized her from the inside out until she finally had to come up for oxygen. The sizzling from the pan didn't compare to the fire burning under her skin. Maybe she wasn't too hungry after all. Maybe they could wait another hour or two. "Your breakfast is going to burn."

"I don't care. I have everything I need right here." He kissed her again, claimed her and everything she'd feared the past three days. Easton had done exactly as he'd promised. He'd helped her forget, just for a little while, but it'd been enough.

A high-powered growl escaped her stomach at the thought of pushing off her body's needs any longer. She pulled back, nearly speechless at the smile coaxing his lips higher. She strengthened her grip on her mug for balance, but Genevieve had been in this man's orbit before. Balance wouldn't come easy. "On second thought, I'll take everything you've cooked so far as long as its soft enough." She eyed the pan as he got back to work flipping eggs. Wait. Not just eggs. "Is that… Is that chocolate in those eggs?"

"Yes, ma'am." He scraped the singed concoction from the pan and settled it onto a nearby plate. "I call it a s'morelet. I saw it on one of the cooking shows. It's your traditional omelet with salt and pepper, but there's marshmallow, chocolate and a bit of crumbled graham cracker inside." He handed her the plate. "Enjoy."

Genevieve accepted the plate. She could already imagine the taste, and it would be anything but a s'more or an omelet. "Okay. I'll take everything you've cooked so far. Except that."

"This is the only thing I've cooked." He handed her a fork, his eyes glittering with humor. "It's this or crossing the very public space between this cabin and the main cabin for breakfast with my mom, Weston and Chloe. In that blanket."

She used the side of her fork to cut into the semicircle shape. Spearing the almost solid bite, Genevieve brought it to her mouth. "Is there another option?"

"It can't be that bad. The chef who came up with it is on the biggest food network in the country." Easton grabbed the fork from her and shoved the entire bite in his mouth. The muscles along his jaw ticked as he chewed, but within a few seconds, his expression contorted into something unrecognizable.

He groaned and spit the mouthful into the sink. Turning on the water, he rinsed over and over. Finished, he swiped at his mouth with the back of his hand. "Yeah, I don't recommend you eat that."

She calmly set the plate back onto the counter and secured the blanket around her chest. "In that case, I suggest you cross the very public space between this cabin and the main cabin to get my breakfast from your mom, Weston and Chloe. In that apron."

Defeat cascaded down his spine as he tossed a kitchen towel to the counter. "I'll be back in a few minutes."

"Thank you." Genevieve studied her rugged reserve officer through the small window over the kitchen sink. The phone she'd purchased before leaving Alamosa reported temperatures close to midtwenties. Served him right for trying to poison the name of s'more. Clinging to the bedspread she clutched around her, she made her way back to the couch and fell into the cushions. She could still smell him on her skin. That authentic blend of Easton and wild. Purely him. It was the same scent she'd breathe in every day he'd finished with his chores around the property. Dirt, pine and fresh air. It was the same scent she hadn't been able to get out of her mind after she'd left Battle Mountain. Her smile fell. How long would it take this time?

Because despite the connection they'd shared last

night, nothing had changed between them. She'd go back to her life in Alamosa, and Easton would still be here. His mother needed him, Weston needed him, this town needed him. No matter how good it'd felt to have him—to counter the emotional loneliness she'd felt for so long—she'd fallen into the same pattern as she had at nineteen years old. She could feel herself getting swept off her feet by him all over again instead of standing on her own.

She bit down on her thumbnail, watching the flames dance back and forth in the fireplace. She'd given up everything to break ties with Battle Mountain. She'd left her family here, moved into a town she'd never visited, put herself through law school and made something of herself. Why then had it been so easy to let him under her skin? What did that say about her?

The front door swung open, and a burst of cold air followed him inside. Balancing two plates in his hands, he kicked the door behind him with his bare heel. "Breakfast—that I did not make—is served."

"Mmm, I'm starving." The heaviness of her thoughts instantly slipped to the back of her mind as Easton rounded the small kitchen table and offered her a plate. Hash browns, scrambled eggs, bacon, sausage, pancakes. Everything she could want or need. He collapsed onto the couch beside her. "It's nearly twenty degrees out there, but you knew that, didn't you?"

"I had to make an example out of you. Don't mess with breakfast food." Genevieve forked a soft mound of hash browns with ketchup into her mouth and melted back against the couch.

"Could you at least share your blanket? All the other ones are cold," he said.

"I'm sure I could be persuaded, given the fact you had a taste of your own—what did you call it?— s'morelet." She set her plate on the arm of the couch and untucked the corner of the blanket from between her breasts. "And that you probably had to answer a whole lot of questions from your family about exactly who the other plate was for."

"I convinced them I was hungrier than usual," he said.

"How did that go over?" Her breathing turned shallow as he swept his gaze down the length of her neck and chest.

"I think my mom is on to us, but I have Weston's word he hasn't said anything. Can't say as much for Chloe." Easton tugged the blanket from around her and tucked himself inside. Pressing her flat onto the couch, he traced his nose along the shell of her ear. "Don't be surprised if my mother shows up at the front door demanding her dishes back to get a glimpse of the woman I'm hiding in my cabin."

Her heartbeat flooded between her ears. Their exhales combined between them, mixing until she wasn't sure where his began and hers ended. "I'd like to believe she wouldn't do that, but I've been around your family long enough now to know otherwise."

"It's only a matter of time really." He skimmed his teeth along her jaw, and an earthquake epicentered low in her belly. Easton followed the curve of her neck with his mouth, leaving her desperate and gasping. "So we shouldn't waste another minute. You know, to keep ourselves from being scarred for the rest of our natural lives."

Genevieve hauled the neck of his apron over his head. Her skin met his, and an explosion of need took control. She fanned her hands over his hips, trying to loosen the tie at his back, but the apron wouldn't budge. "I agree."

Two knocks was all the warning they had before the front door swung open. "I knew you weren't that hungry."

Genevieve froze as a different kind of heat flared up her neck and into her face.

Easton's forehead collapsed onto her collarbones. "Genevieve, you remember my mother, don't you?"

Craning her head back to center Karie Ford in her vision, Genevieve untucked her hand from around the woman's son and extended it in greeting. "Nice to see you again, Mrs. Ford."

"Easton James Ford. Here I thought your father and I had taught you better than to look for trouble." Karie Ford waited for them to get decent, her back to them. The tendons in her neck protested under strain, but it was her tone that raised the hairs on the back of Easton's neck. He knew that tone well. Every time he and Weston had stepped out of line growing up. The voice of doom. That, combined with the use of his full name, clenched every muscle he owned. "Your father is probably rolling over in his grave, young man. Don't you have any respect for yourself?"

"I think you're about to get grounded." Genevieve buttoned her red silk blouse she'd worn a couple nights ago, the scrubs from the hospital crumpled near the fireplace. She tried to fight the smile curling the corners of her mouth but failed. The flush of pink coloring her cheeks stood stark against her pale skin. Absolutely beautiful.

"At least you knocked." Easton threaded his hands through his T-shirt and pulled it into place. He noted a black stretch of lace across the couch and handed Genevieve's bra off to her before his mother had a chance to turn around. "It could've been a lot worse."

"It could've been a lot worse? That's all you have to say about the fact you're sleeping with the woman who left you at the altar?" His mother turned sea-blue eyes—the same color as his—onto him. Most of his life, he'd been entranced by their warmth, but the past few months, there was a solidity to them he recognized in his own. Losing her spouse had changed Karie Ford from the strong matriarch he'd always known into little more than a husk of the woman she'd been all his life. She tried to hide it, the cracks in her armor, but in this instance, like recognized like.

Weston hiked up the two stairs and across the threshold, slightly out of breath. "Mom, the hash browns started burning. You set off the smoke detector. What are you—" His brother scanned the scene, from the discarded plates of food, to Genevieve buttoning her slacks and the pile of blankets in front of the fireplace. A deep laugh resonated through the small cabin as Chloe peered around her fiancé. "Oh, I get it. She lost her earring, and you were helping her find it."

Genevieve's hands shot to her ears. "I did lose an earring." She searched through the blanket on the couch then moved on to shoving her hands between the cushions.

"What's a single moment of privacy if it doesn't turn into a family affair." Easton ran one hand through his hair, but he wasn't about to be scolded for bringing a woman back to his place. He wasn't a teenager who'd only been thinking with his second brain. At least, not completely. He scooped one of the couch pillows off the floor and threw it at Weston's face. "You guys are the worst."

His brother caught it. "I'm not the one wearing an apron."

"You have a point." Easton tried to untie the strings around his waist but ended up ripping the apron clean off instead. "Problem fixed."

"It's all fun and games until someone gets hurt." Karie Ford's ear-length white-blond hair fell from its usual style into her face. She pushed it back, exasperation clear in her aged expression. Closing in on her early sixties, the woman was a tornado of authority and confidence. His mother's delicate jaw turned hard. In reality, there wasn't much else delicate about Karie Ford. Her dark jeans and a flannel shirt highlighted a strength Easton had relied on a lot over the years, the kind she got from working the land around them going on thirty-five years. Her laugh lines deepened around her eyes and mouth as she glared. Sobering him up faster than a straight black cup of coffee or a single touch from Genevieve ever could.

"Mom, it's not that big of a deal. Genevieve asked me to consult on one of her cases a few days ago." He wasn't sure why he felt the need to explain other than he needed them to see this was a good thing, that he'd let go of the anger and betrayal, and was attempting to move on with his life. "We got to talking. One thing led to another, and—"

"Yes, it looked like a good conversation from what I could see." Karie pointed to the floor. "By the way, dear, you can stop searching the couch. Your earring is over here by my foot."

Genevieve's gaze hit the floor a split second before she shot her head back up. She straightened, smoothing wrinkles from her slacks. A humorless laugh escaped past her kiss-stung lips. She pointed toward the door. "I'll tell you what, you can keep it, and I'll just—"

"You'll stay where you are," Karie said.

"Yep. That's exactly what I thought, too. I'll stay right here." Genevieve interlaced her fingers in front of her. "Great minds think alike."

"Easton, you're a grown man." Karie Ford's attention shifted to Genevieve and back. "Who you… talk to is none of my business. Hell, I'm glad you've found someone to converse with after you've spent the past year moping around, but you need to know what you're going to get yourself into this time. If this conversation is going to end the same as it did last time, I'm not going to stand here and let her hurt this family." His mother set her chin, and Easton braced for the wrath of that one look, the one that could strip him down to nothing. Instead, she turned that look onto Genevieve. "What you did was cow-

ardly, Genevieve Alexander. You should be ashamed
to show yourself in this town. You broke my son's
heart, and because of you Easton felt the need to join
the army. Because of you he was on that damn supply run in the first—"

"That's enough." Easton positioned himself in
front of Genevieve. Blame wouldn't do them any
good. "Mom, you have every right to be mad that I
didn't tell you Genevieve was staying here, but you
have no idea what she's been through. In fact, there's
a lot you don't know, and going all mama bear is only
making it worse. What happened fifteen years ago
happened. Nothing you say or do will ever change
that. If I'm able to let it go, so should you."

Weston and Chloe slowly backed out of the cabin
as the tension physically solidified between him and
his mother.

Karie Ford stepped back, the fine lines around her
mouth deeper than he'd ever seen them before. Grief
did that to a person, changed them from the inside
out. There was no predicting it, no stopping it. The
sufferer was at its mercy, and all they could do now
was hold on for dear life until the weight lifted. "You
want me to forget the look on your face when you
found her engagement ring in that bridal room? How
you disappeared into the woods for nearly two weeks
without a word after you realized she wasn't coming
back? How when you finally came home, you told

us you'd be leaving for basic training the next morning?" A line of tears glittered in his mother's eyes. "Your superior officer had to call me and tell me what'd happened in Afghanistan because you were unconscious for a week after you pulled your unit from the wreckage, and now you're finally home. No. I'm not going to forget, Easton. Because of what she did, I lost my son, and I'm not going to lose you again."

Hell. Easton stepped toward her, his heart heavier than a moment before. The past year played on a black-and-white loop in his head, but the ones with Genevieve had color. Hope. "Mom, you know how hard it's been here for me. As much as I wanted to deny anything was wrong, I need help." Confidence held his head higher. "Genevieve helps me. Okay?"

One second. Two.

"You're right, Karie." Genevieve stepped around him, and it took everything in him not to pull her back. But this woman had never let anyone control her. Why would she start now? "I was a coward. I should've had the guts to tell Easton—to tell all of you—why I had to leave, but I was scared. I didn't think any of you would understand because I wasn't sure I did. I'm sorry. I know my leaving didn't only hurt Easton. It hurt you and your family as well, and there's not a day that goes by that I don't regret that choice. You were like a second mother to me. You were there to help me pick out a wedding dress and made sure I was taking care of myself during all the planning. I'll never be able to repay you for that, but most of all I'm grateful you raised such a strong son. Without him, I wouldn't be standing here."

"If you say she helps with what you're going through, I believe you." Karie nodded once. "Tell me what I can do to help, too."

"Forgetting you walked in on us would be a start," Easton said.

A quirk of a smile tugged at his mother's mouth. She folded her hands in front of her. "Lock the door next time, and bring the dishes back when you're through, for crying out loud. I didn't raise you in a barn." With that, Karie Ford turned and closed the front door behind her.

Genevieve's relieved exhale doubled her over beside him. She pressed her fingers into both eyes. "For the record, I don't think I've ever been more embarrassed in my entire life, and I've had everyone in Battle Mountain stare me down for leaving their golden boy at the altar. I didn't think it could get much worse than that."

"I warned you my conversation with them didn't go well when I was getting us breakfast." Easton pulled her into his side. He kissed her temple, resurrecting a hint of wood smoke and desire. If he was being honest, his mother walking in on him with a woman was probably one of the least embarrassing occurrences. "You might as well get used to it now. This is the first of many embarrassments for us in the future."

Genevieve straightened under his touch. "The future?"

His phone pinged with an incoming message. Releasing her, he crossed the small cabin and scooped it off the kitchen counter where the dying evidence of his attempt to be charming lay in shambles. He swallowed as his gag reflux kicked in. Eggs did not mix well with chocolate. He'd never make that mistake again. He tapped the new message.

"It's Weston." A spike of adrenaline lightninged through him. Tearing his gaze from the phone, he focused on Genevieve. "He got a call from Captain Morsey. Laila Ballard just walked into the medical center on her own two feet, claiming Lieutenant Parrish abducted her." His phone threatened to crack under his grip. "She's alive."

Chapter Eleven

Genevieve's fingers shook as she wrapped her hand around the door handle. Knocking, she shouldered inside and faced the woman she'd turned into a target. "Laila."

White gauze matted a halo of stringy brown hair. An oxygen tube strung across a weathered face. Dark eyes, the color of coal, quickly dried as Laila Ballard realized she wasn't alone. Two lacerations cut through a thin bottom lip, but the Contractor's latest victim still had enough strength to sit higher in the bed. Small stains of blood filtered through the wrapping around her left ear. Her low, slightly distorted voice barely carried across the private room. "Ms. Alexander, I wasn't expecting you."

"Genevieve." She closed the heavy door as quietly as possible so as not to alarm her friend, but firsthand experience warned her it'd take a lot more than a few niceties to help Laila process what she'd been through. Laila had been abducted because of her connection to Genevieve. There was no easy fix for something like that. No Hallmark card that expressed the guilt and sorrow raging inside. *Sorry you were abducted and dismembered. Thinking of you.* She scanned the array of flowers and stuffed animals on the table beside Laila. "How are you?"

"Oh, you know. It's a little harder to hear nowadays, but what do you think of my new accessory?" Laila tugged at the wrap of gauze keeping infection at bay. Thin fingers picked at invisible specs in the sheets as Genevieve took her seat beside the bed. Flourescent lighting glinted off the spread of scalpels, tweezers and other surgical tools on a rolling tray a few feet away. "When I gave my statement to Captain Morsey, he told me the man who took me, who did this..." She motioned to her ear. "He's the same one who killed all those other women? The one who broke into your house before you borrowed my car?"

"Yes." She nodded, her chin wobbling. This woman had already been through so much. Losing her daughter so violently had nearly broken her. If it hadn't been for the trial giving her something to fight for, something to focus on, Genevieve wasn't sure the grieving mother would've made it. Now this. She reached for her friend's hand. For connection, for comfort, for a direct conduit to express everything she couldn't say. "Laila, I'm sorry. I thought I was being careful, but if it hadn't been for me, Lieutenant Parrish wouldn't have—"

"No sense in talking about things we can't change." Cool, papery skin countered the anger churning in her gut as Laila laid her hand over Genevieve's. Laila couldn't be much older than her late forties, early fifties, but she'd aged in a matter of days. Violence did that. It took the best parts of someone's being and wrung them out to dry, leaving nothing but emptiness and isolation. The ends of Laila's hair frayed around her face. Apart from the obvious damage to her ear, she had seemingly only suffered minor bruises and scrapes. Nurses had cleaned the blood from her skin, but Genevieve could still pick out debris in those dark curls. "Tell me about this police officer who's been helping you with the investigation."

"Easton?" How had she known about…? Captain Morsey must've told her. Genevieve tried to tamp the urge to fidget for a distraction, but the truth was plain to see. She cared about him. She squeezed Laila's hand. "He's a friend. We knew each other way back. In fact, we were engaged to be married before I came to Alamosa. I asked him to wait outside so we could talk alone."

A knowing smile thinned battered lips, and discomfort flared in Genevieve's chest. Laila pressed the oxygen tube harder against her nose and closed her eyes for a moment. "I appreciate that. As much as I'd love the chance to meet him for myself, I'm not dressed for company at the moment."

"You look great. Think of it this way. Now you can stop looking for all those single earrings you lost over the years." She shook her head at her own joke. "Too soon?"

"A little." A strangled breath pinned Laila to the bed for a series of seconds, and the woman clamped down on her hand. Hard. Exhaustion wrecked the once full cheeks and flawless skin under Laila's eyes. New lines carved between her eyebrows as she stared up at the ceiling. She'd been through a lot. It would take time to recover, but she would recover. One day her abduction wouldn't be the first thing she thought of in the morning, just as Genevieve hoped it wouldn't be for her.

"My friend I was telling you about, Easton, he was a soldier overseas up until about a year ago. His unit was on their way to make a supply run when they hit an IED. He was the only one who survived, but to this day, he still struggles with what happened." She hadn't meant to spill Easton's secret, but the buried terror in Laila's gaze, the vulnerability and unknown of what lay ahead, urged her to make this right any way she could. "He's only recently started talking about what he deals with on a daily basis, but it's changed him for the better. Do you want to tell me what happened?"

Laila closed her eyes again, turning her head away. "The police needed my statement, especially given one of their own was involved, but… I don't want to remember."

"I understand." Genevieve set her free hand over Laila's, sandwiching the woman's cool, onion-thin skin between hers. "You don't have to talk, but just know, I'm here. Okay? Whatever you need, I'll be here. I'll help you get through this. No matter what it takes."

The once stone-hardened mother Genevieve had studied in court during her daughter's killer's trial had vanished, and in her place, was a woman who'd never be the same again. Laila turned back, warm eyes locking on their intertwined hands on the edge of the bed. "You were always so kind to me. Always there when things got hard." Laila nodded. "It was dark in the house when he came in. I didn't hear him over the sound of the television. I have to turn it up so loud these days, but I felt a draft. I got up off the couch to make sure I hadn't left a window open, and there he was, standing there in the middle of the hallway. He stared at me like I was expecting him. Next thing I knew I was zip-tied by the wrists and ankles in some place I didn't recognize."

"You don't remember anything from when you were taken to when you woke up?" she asked.

"No." Laila shook her head. "But he was there. The same man. Lieutenant Parrish. He'd been waiting for me to wake up. He had a knife in one hand, told me he needed me to help him send a message." The woman's expression contorted in remembered pain, and Genevieve squeezed her hand again. "He took out my hearing aid and cut off my ear. I must've passed out because when I woke up again, he was gone. I don't know how long. I told myself the next time he came back I'd be ready, that I needed to stay strong for my baby."

Tears streaked down her hollow cheeks. "One of the floorboards was loose. I managed to pry it up and use one of the nails to cut through the zip ties around my wrists, but before I could get free, I heard his vehicle. I hid the nail in my hand and pretended I was still tied up, but when he got close to give me a drink of water, I stabbed him in the side of the neck. There was so much blood, but I couldn't stop. I cut through the ties around my ankles, and I ran as fast as I could until I got back to town."

Genevieve's pulse ticked harder behind her ears as she tried to superimpose Parrish's face over the masked man who'd hung her from a tree in the middle of the woods.

"You were so brave. If you hadn't killed him, you

might've ended up like those other women." Genevieve rubbed her hand along Laila's forearm, but a knot of hesitation clenched her gut. She didn't remember a whole lot about the minutes after the Contractor had caught up with her in the dunes, but there was one detail that stood out more than the others.

The killer had never showed her his face.

Her stomach soured. Why would Parrish have let Laila see his then? That didn't make sense. No. Something wasn't right about her story. She licked her lips to counter the physical signs Easton had always been able to pick up on when she lied and soothed her friend's hand again. "And Lieutenant Parrish wasn't wearing a mask, right? Just like he didn't when he took the other victims?"

Laila swiped at her face to catch the tears that'd escaped. "That's right. I recognized him immediately. I figured he'd planned on killing me, so why hide his face if I wasn't going to live long enough to identify him?"

Oxygen squeezed from her lungs. Genevieve struggled to keep her expression neutral. Laila was lying about the abduction. Why? She'd been through a physical trauma. Was she agreeing because she wanted this over with, or had Parrish forgone the mask specially for his latest victim? "I'm so glad you're okay now. Thank you for sharing with me. I think I'm going to let you rest for a bit. You've had a hard few days."

Another strangled breath filled the silence between them. Laila pointed toward the bathroom. "Could you fill up my mug with water first, please?"

"Of course." Genevieve patted her friend's hand, collected the empty oversized water mug with bendy straw from the bedside table and crossed to the other side of the room. Streaming water echoed in her ears inside the small bathroom, but the door had closed enough to block Laila's view of her. She let the water run a bit longer than necessary to sort through the details. Why would the Contractor reveal who he was to Laila when he'd gone out of his way to make sure Genevieve could never identify him at the dunes? They'd theorized he'd cut off Laila's ear to lure her to the woman's home and give him a chance to abduct Genevieve. But if he'd been using Laila to send a message as she'd said, why cut off her ear when Elisa Johnson's body had done the job?

She'd used up enough time. Turning off the water, she popped the lid back onto the mug labeled with the medical center's logo and returned to the main room. Laila hadn't moved as far as she could tell, but the way her friend studied her pooled dread at the base of her spine. Something was wrong. Genevieve set the mug on the bedside table. "Here you go. Anything else I can get for you?"

"It's getting hard to talk." Laila motioned her closer, her voice strained and weak. More so than a minute ago. "Come closer. There's something I forgot to tell you."

Genevieve took a single step closer. Only to realize the neatly organized surgical tools on the cart a few feet away had been disturbed.

One was missing.

A vivid awareness bled into Laila's gaze. She ripped her arm from beneath the sheets and arced the scalpel in her hand down.

A SHRILL RING filled his ears.

Easton checked the phone's caller ID as his candy bar from the clinic's waiting room vending machine fell. He answered on the third ring. "You find anything at the scene where Laila Ballard said she was being held?"

"Well, Lieutenant Parrish is dead. So that's something." Weston lowered his voice, most likely to contain information if he was still outside the crime scene. A search of the lieutenant's financials and property records hadn't produced a lead to narrow the manhunt, but one of the other victim's vacation cabin had served his purposes. The bastard had held Laila Ballard for three days with little sustenance or care for the damage he'd done to her ear. It was amazing she hadn't died from infection. "There's a rusted nail sticking out of his jugular. The medical examiner says he would've bled out in a matter of minutes. Would you like me to be more specific than that?"

"Damn it." He should've known. The proximity of Parrish's cabin to the scene where he'd found Genevieve hanging from a tree, the fact the lieutenant had disappeared off the radar after learning where he and Genevieve would be staying the night—it'd all been there. He and Genevieve had been closing in, and Parrish had upped the stakes. "What else?"

"The crime scene unit recovered two sets of severed zip ties lined with blood. Most likely your vic's, but Alamosa PD is having the DNA tested to confirm along with all the other samples of blood. Parrish's boots match the prints Alamosa cast from the abduction scene and Genevieve's home. Same size, same tread. I can tell you this is where he kept her for the past three days. I've got protein bar wrappers, empty water bottles, a bucket in the corner and a gag. We also recovered a blade that could've been used to cut her ear off. He was keeping her alive for some reason, and there are plenty more supplies here that makes me think he wasn't finished with her yet," Weston said. "From what I see here, she fought back. Hard. Aside from the arterial spray from the lieutenant here, there are clear signs of a struggle, but there's one thing I can't explain."

"What's that?" Easton asked.

"Laila Ballard told the captain she had to pry a floorboard free to access the nail she used to cut herself loose and kill Parrish." Heavy footsteps penetrated through the line. "I've been over every inch of this place. There aren't any loose floorboards."

"That doesn't make sense." Where else would the nail have come from?

A scream singed down every nerve ending he owed.

"Easton?" Weston's voice notched higher.

"I'll call you back." Easton sprinted down the hallway toward Laila Ballard's room and barged inside. The door slammed into the wall behind it as he faced off with both women, one wielding a scalpel. "Genevieve!"

She'd managed to catch Laila Ballard's wrist before the blade struck, but the fight in her shoulders said their victim was much stronger than she'd led police and hospital staff to believe. A growl escaped her throat as she threw Laila's arm out to the side, and she stumbled backward into the wall behind her.

A homicidal glaze had transformed the victim who'd walked into the emergency room just a few hours ago into an unrecognizable force. Rage contorted beaten features as Laila Ballard lunged. The scalpel curved downward toward Genevieve. "She's dead because of you!"

Easton threw her out of the way. The blade sliced down the length of his arm. Agony forced him to suck air between his teeth. Protest rumbled through his chest, but Laila wasn't stopping. He had to get control of the blade. Footsteps and shouts echoed down the hallway. Security must've heard the commotion and come running. Good. Because the woman on the other side of the blade wouldn't go down without a fight.

"Laila, stop! We can help you." Genevieve held her palms out in surrender. "You just have to tell us what really happened during your abduction."

Heavy inhales strained the victim's chest as she latched onto the end of the bed for balance. That dark gaze never left her target, but it was only a matter of time before Easton would be forced to take her down. Sweat beaded along the woman's temples and neck. "You. You were supposed to make sure that drunk never made bail. You are the reason my daughter is dead. If it wasn't for you, he never would've gotten behind that wheel again. My baby would still be here instead of the cemetery."

Genevieve's gasp filled the space between them. "I tried, Laila. You know that. The judge—"

"Will get what's coming to her." Spittle flew from thin, battered lips. "But first, you're going to pay for what you did to me. You all will."

Every muscle down Easton's back hardened in

battle-ready defense. Awareness told him security had arrived, but he motioned for them to hold off. They could still get out of this without any casualties. He could still get Genevieve out of here. "Laila, put the scalpel down. You haven't hurt anybody. You can still walk away from this. We can help you."

"Shut up!" Laila Ballard angled the blade in his direction. Sobs wracked though her chest, hiking her shoulders up and down in short bursts. "Just shut up." She turned her drowning gaze back to Genevieve. "He wanted to help me. That's why he killed them. He did it for me, but you…you wouldn't die."

"The other victims, you mean. The Contractor killed them for you?" Genevieve's voice softened and understanding filled her expression. "Annette Scofield was the EMT on scene that day of the accident. She was the one who pulled your daughter from the car. In her report, your daughter was still breathing, but she died on her way to the hospital. You blame Annette for not being able to save her. And Ruby Wagner?"

"She was the responding officer." Laila's anger lessened as grief took its place. "My daughter was in the car. She was alive, but the police did nothing until the EMTs arrived. Officer Wagner let my baby suffer because she was too untrained to know how to get her out of the car. She could've saved her life!"

Genevieve lowered her hands to her sides, taking

a single step forward. "And Elise Johnson was my assistant. She helped me file the charges against the man who got behind that wheel, but it didn't stop him from doing it again. From killing your daughter in the accident."

"Genevieve." Easton swallowed the urge to reach out for her, to pull her back to safety, but she took another step. His blood pressure skyrocketed into dangerous territory, and he lowered his hand from holding off security. One wrong move. That was all it would take. He'd grab Genevieve and let security do their jobs. All that mattered was her.

"You all failed her. Why should you get to live when she doesn't?" Laila asked. "Why do you get to go through the rest of your lives like nothing happened when I'm barely surviving mine?"

"I understand. All of it. You have every right to blame me, but the others? They didn't deserve what the Contractor did to them, Laila. They were good people. They had families and dreams and their entire lives ahead of them." Genevieve held her chin level with the floor, no trace of fear in her eyes. "You said he killed them for you. Do you mean Lieutenant Parrish? Why? What does he owe you?"

Laila shook her head. The scalpel wobbled in her hand as her arm grew tired, and Easton shifted his weight onto his toes. The next time she got distracted, he'd make his move. "It doesn't matter." The victim centered cold, dark eyes on Genevieve. "All that's left is for me to hold up my end of the deal."

Laila Ballard turned the blade on herself.

"No!" Genevieve lunged, but it was too late. The damage had already been done.

Easton threaded his hands between her ribs and arms and hauled her back into his chest as security and emergency personnel rushed into the room. Chaos filled the space as he maneuvered Genevieve through the door and down the hallway. She fought his hold, wanting to go back, but there was nothing she could do. Her sobs shook through him as he angled her into the waiting room. The image of the grieving mother slicing through her own jugular burned into his brain, and Easton closed his eyes against the violence of it all. He forced himself to concentrate on the curve of Genevieve's shoulder, the way she smelled, the rhythm of her heart beating against his. Her sobs quieted after a few minutes, but still, she didn't move.

"I could've helped her." She buried her nose in the crook of his neck.

The heaviness of that statement settled on his chest. "I'm not sure anyone could have, Genevieve. She was hurting. All she wanted was her daughter back, and you couldn't make that happen. No matter how hard you tried."

"Why didn't I know she was in so much pain?

Why didn't I see the connection between the victims before now?" she asked.

"Alamosa's a small town. You, Elise, Annette, Ruby—you've all worked a number of cases together. We were looking for a needle in a haystack that dated back years." He smoothed her hair back away from her face. "You did everything you could. You know that. Some people just don't want to be helped. They go through their lives lying to their loved ones, hanging on to the past like it's a lifeline. Hell, they even lie to themselves, but it only makes things worse. Until Laila was ready to accept help, her future looked exactly like this. She made the choice. Not you or anyone else. She chose this."

He knew that better than most, and Easton couldn't help but wonder if his future would've mirrored Laila Ballard's if Genevieve hadn't come back into his life. How much longer would he have suffered with nothing to believe in or show for it without her?

"She was going to kill me." Genevieve straightened. Tears dried in crusted lines down her face, streaking black mascara along the way. Some color had come back into her face, but it would take a while before the memories didn't hurt so much. "Guess that means I don't have to worry about getting her car back to her."

"Always looking for that silver lining." Easton

swiped at her cheeks with the pad of his thumb, ignoring the pain down his arm. Damn, she was beautiful, and honest, and warm. Everything he wasn't. Everything he needed. He memorized the fullness of her lips, the flawlessness of her skin and wisdom in her eyes. Merely a little more than three decades on earth but more than a lifetime of understanding and perspective in the emerald depths. "That's why I love you."

Chapter Twelve

Love?

Genevieve angled away from his chest, and his touch slipped from her skin. Her heart rate ticked up a notch, blood draining from her face. No. That wasn't... That wasn't possible. "What do you mean you love me? We've only been working this case for three days."

"I mean exactly what I said," he said. "You might think it's only been three days, but I've loved you since the first moment I met you all those years go, Genevieve. I never stopped, even after you left. I knew. I knew I was going to spend the rest of my life with you."

She forced her legs to support her as she backed away. She didn't know what to say to that, what to think. Her decision to return to Battle Mountain had strictly been to ask Easton help in figuring out who'd broken into her home and murdered her assistant. Not to get involved with him all over again. They'd worked this case together, and while it'd been comforting and assuring to have him at her side, she wasn't ready for…this.

Her chest felt too tight. It was getting harder to breathe. Thank goodness she was still standing in the middle of the hospital. "What do you expect me to say to that, Easton? I've been running on nothing but adrenaline and fear since someone broke into my home. I just learned friend has been using a serial killer to exact her revenge on the people she blames for her daughter's death. I just watched her slice open her throat with a scalpel in front of me because she failed. Four women attributed to the Contractor are dead—possibly five if Laila doesn't survive—and you're telling me you want to spend the rest of your life with me. It's a little much to take."

Easton closed the distance between them, every ounce the ranch hand, the solider and the police officer she'd believed him to be. "I understand that, but I know exactly what Laila Ballard went through. I've spent the past fifteen years of my life denying anything that might've brought me pain. I was on the same path as she was, letting all that anger and betrayal build up. I ran as far and as fast as I could from the people who cared about me the most to make sure I couldn't be hurt again, and the only thing it got me was more pain."

Her gut clenched.

He trailed his fingers up her arms. "Then you came

back, and you…you made me realize I'm more than what's happened to me. You made me realize I could take these experiences and use them for something good. I could help people. I wouldn't have considered the idea if it hadn't been for you. I would've finished this investigation, gone back into hiding and let you slip away again. But I don't want to be that man, Genevieve. I'm better when I'm with you. Stay. Please. Once this investigation is finished, we can get our own place on a ranch, in Battle Mountain or here—wherever you want. We can finally give this a shot."

She believed him. Sincerity laced every word, and there was no doubt about the changes she'd seen in him over the course of this investigation. He'd let his guard down, for her, but the knot of uncertainty, of having to make a choice right here, right now, tightened in her gut. Genevieve intertwined her fingers with his and held his hands to her chest. Despite the amount of crying she'd done in the course of forty-eight hours, tears burned in her eyes. "I'm glad you were able to find some healing during our time together, Easton. You have no idea how much it means to me, and I'm so honored I got to be here to watch it happen." She internally fortified herself. He'd finally found healing, and she was about to destroy it all. Again. "But I've already given this a shot."

"I don't understand." He slipped his fingers from hers, leaving her cold and alone as he stepped out of reach. Confusion deepened the lines between his brows and softened the sharp angles of his features. In that moment, he wasn't the soldier she'd envisioned or even the law enforcement officer who'd protected her. He was that barely-graduated teenager she'd lost herself in all those years ago.

"I came to Battle Mountain for your help, and I can't thank you enough for everything you've done. If it weren't for you, I wouldn't have made it out of those woods. I know that, and I'm not sure I'll ever be able to repay you for it, but..." She bit the inside of her mouth to keep herself from shutting down. "Falling into whatever this is between us, pretending we can pick up where we left off—I'm not ready for that. I thought I was, but I can feel myself getting completely wrapped up in you again, your way of life, your personality, your family, and I've fought too hard to be my own person to give it all up now."

"So, what? We go back to the way things were? Like nothing happened between us?" His voice broke, and her heart crumpled right along with it. "Once this case is finished, you'll come back to Alamosa, and I'll go back to Battle Mountain, and we just carry on with our lives?"

"I think it's better if we end it now." It was the only way. "I know you're invested in seeing this case through, but Alamosa PD has a connection between the victims now. It's over. Parrish is dead. If Laila survives, they can question her to sure up their case. You and Weston and Dr. Miles got us this far, but there's nothing more you can do here. You're officially off the hook."

"Off the hook." Easton scrubbed a hand down his face, turning his back to her. "It's that easy for you, isn't it? To walk away. I should've known you'd use me for what you needed and run. That's what you're good at, right?"

"No. That's not..." His words hit her as though she'd taken a physical punch to the gut. Oxygen crushed from her lungs, and she slid her palms over her midsection to somehow keep herself together. "Easton, I care about you. A lot, but that's not enough to drop everything and ride off into the sunset to live happily ever after. We have to consider each other's needs. I'm not a teenager anymore who will compromise what I want because that's what's expected of me."

"Then why are you still acting like one? You can't tell me this is all about your insecurity. You're the district attorney, for crying out loud." Shock at his own accusation smoothed his expression and parted his mouth, and the fight seemed to leave him right there in the middle of the hospital waiting room. "I don't just care about you, Genevieve. I love you, damn it. That has to be worth something to you."

Genevieve slipped her fingers into her slacks, all

too aware of the eyes and ears of the hospital staff waiting for her next response. She directed her attention to the floor. Her insecurity. That was exactly what this was all about. Because no matter how many times she'd wished she could go back and change things between them, there would always be part of her that wouldn't feel worthy of him. A part of her that believed he'd worked out how to find that equal balance they needed that she couldn't, that she could be as casual and confident as he was.

Genevieve clamped her mouth shut, forcing herself to take a deep breath. The same feelings of doubt and self-consciousness that stereotyped her as a young woman still held weight. They still deserved to be respected, and so did she. She wasn't a teenager, and she didn't have to stand here and listen to him echo his own insecurities back at her. She had enough of her own. He was right about one thing. His love should've counted for something, but in her case, it wouldn't ever be enough.

She crossed one foot behind her, ready to flee before she shattered into a million pieces right there in the middle of the waiting room. "I think it's best if I leave. I'll get a ride from one of the Alamosa PD officers outside. Please, Easton, take care of yourself. Okay? Don't let this stop you from finding peace."

Shame broke through the last of her fortifications as she darted down the hallway. A flatline warning escaped the crack of Laila Ballard's room as doctors tried to bring her back. Genevieve slammed against the side exit door and shoved out into the blistering night. A chill ran up the length of her arms. She'd left her coat in Easton's truck, but she didn't have the courage to go back to face him for the keys. She ran her hands up and down her bare arms. She'd left her bag at his cabin too, but there wasn't anything in there that couldn't be replaced. Easton had returned her keys after her release from the hospital, and she'd luckily slipped them into her pocket instead of her overnight bag. All she needed was a ride to her house, and she could put the investigation behind her. Put Easton behind her.

She'd done it once. She could do it again.

Lieutenant Parrish was dead. The case was closed. She could move on with her life.

Genevieve rounded the side of the medical center and targeted one of the Alamosa patrol cruisers. She picked up the pace as she crossed the semicircle drive in front of the emergency room and flagged down the officer behind the wheel. Recognition flared as he stepped from the car, and a surge of relief chased back the pressure behind her sternum. "Mind if I catch a ride back to my house? That is, if it's been cleared as a crime scene by now?"

"Don't mind at all, Counselor." Chief Morsey collapsed back into his seat, a to-go coffee cup in his hand. He positioned it into the center console as she wrenched open the passenger side door and climbed inside. The heater was already running, filling the small space with a hint of cologne. "I've been out at the scene where Parrish was holding Laila Ballard all day. Just heard from her doctor about what happened with her. It's a damn shame. Ford decide to stick around to see if she recovers?"

"Something like that." Genevieve strapped into her seatbelt, attention honed through the windshield. It was stupid to fantasize about Easton running through the sliding glass double doors and stopping her from leaving, but she couldn't help herself. He'd always been her knight in shining armor when she'd needed him. Now it was time to be her own. She pressed back into the warm seat as they pulled away from the hospital. "Thank you, Captain. I'm sure you're just as glad this case is over as I am."

He moved so fast, she wasn't entirely sure what'd happened until pain lightninged across her neck. One hand steady on the wheel, Captain Morsey pinned her to the seat with a blade pressed angrily to her throat. "Who says it's over?"

GENEVIEVE WAS GONE.

He stood there in the middle of the waiting room, his reflection blurred in the window of the vending machine. The pressure building behind his sternum reached a crescendo. He'd given her everything these past few days, but it hadn't been enough. He would never be enough for her. She'd been the woman he'd relied on to help him heal. Now what was he supposed to do? Go back to his cabin, to his isolation?

Without her, he was losing his grip. The process was already starting. How long before the emptiness came for him? How long before he was completely alone? He studied the face staring back at him as failure consumed him from the inside. Numbness threatened to overtake his control. Easton leveraged his weight against the frame of the vending machine and set his head against the glass.

A soft ringing started in his ears. His breath fogged in front of him. Not enough to keep him anchored in the moment. Easton forced himself to take a deep breath, but the harder he reached for that control, the faster it slipped away. Images of pain, of fear and loss splintered his consciousness in two, but instead of sand and fire, there was only Genevieve. The desperation to find her after he realized she'd been taken from Laila Ballard's home, the lack of color in her skin when he'd found her hanging from a tree. Each memory twisted and folded into an unrecognizable torrent of emotion he couldn't regulate on his own. Not without her.

His fist penetrated the glass window.

It shattered around his hand and hit the industrial

carpet. Pain rippled up through his forearm, and he squeezed his hand into a fist. Blood bloomed through the small lacerations across his skin. He'd survived his fiancée leaving, an ambush on his unit and the murder of his father. How much more was he supposed to take before it was okay to give up?

Easton stepped back from the vending machine. He tugged his cell phone free. Blood spread across the screen as he scrolled through his contacts. He hit the one he needed and brought the phone to his ear. Three rings. Four. The call went to voicemail, as he'd predicted it would, and he sank back into one of the chairs behind him. He closed his eyes to focus on the voice on the other end.

Hey, this is James Ford. I'm probably available right now, but I can't find my phone. Leave a message, and we'll see if I remember how to access voicemail when I find it.

The line beeped, and Easton didn't know what else to do other than to follow this through. "Hey, Dad. Guess I don't have to worry about showing you how to check your voicemail anymore. I lost count of how many times you'd shown up at my door asking for my help when we both knew you didn't need it. You were there to check on me, to see if I needed you, but I was an idiot who thought I could do this on my own. I need you now, Dad." His voice cracked as sorrow wrung him dry. "I need you to tell me what to do next."

He lowered the phone into his lap and hit End. James Ford wasn't going to call back. He wasn't ever going to hear the message. He wasn't ever going to show up on Easton's doorstep pretending he was too old to figure out technology on his own. Easton stared at the shattered remnants of the vending machine window. The man had taught him responsibility, reliance and loyalty, but in the end, his father had died for being selfless.

His phone rang.

Every nerve ending he owned caught fire at the name scrolling across his screen. James Ford (Dad). Impossible. Inhale shaky, he answered the call. "Yeah?"

"Easton." His mother's voice penetrated through the thick haze of betrayal and grief. Grief of losing his father, of not being strong enough to save his unit, of Genevieve walking out on him all over again.

"You didn't disconnect Dad's phone." He swiped at his face, realizing too late his hand was still bleeding from the vending machine and the other from the swipe of Laila Ballard's scalpel.

"No. I still call it when I need to hear his voice. I won't tell you how many times a day that's getting to be lately." The soft, familiar click of knitting needles hitting against one another filled the other side of the line. He recounted Sunday mornings in front of the television—he, Weston and his father glued to whatever mutant superhero episode had come on, while his mother knitted silently in the recliner behind them. Those mornings hadn't been exceptional, but they'd been everything to him. "Sounds like you needed to hear him, too."

A burst of pain and laughter shattered the last hold on his control, and Easton leveraged his elbows against his knees. He pinched his forehead between his index finger and thumb, trying to rub the shame away. "I don't know why. I know he's gone. There's no changing that."

"Honey, I don't call this number expecting your father to pick up the phone and start talking to me like nothing happened." The sound of his mother's knitting needles ceased. "I do it because hearing his voice makes me feel like I'm not alone. Sure, I have you and Weston and Chloe here from time to time, but you've each got your own lives, and there's no shame in searching for things that make us feel better. Even if no one else understands it."

His instincts gave him the distinct impression Karie Ford wasn't talking about calling a ghost anymore. The barriers that'd kept him from exposing his greatest weakness shattered as violently as the vending machine glass a few feet away. "Everyone I care about leaves. My unit, Dad, Genevieve. Weston and

Chloe are starting their lives. They'll get married and want a place of their own, a family. As much as I hate to think about it, you're not going to be around forever. Soon enough, it'll just be me." There was no denying the truth as it exploded to the surface. "How am I going to get better if I don't have anyone left, Mom?"

Silence filtered through the line. One second. Two. "Maybe you don't—"

"Officer Ford, we managed to get Laila Ballard stable," an unfamiliar voice said.

He craned his head up. A physician caught sight of the vending machine and the bloody smears down Easton's arm. Bringing the phone back to his ear, Easton nodded. "Mom, I'm going to have to call you back."

"I'm going to hold you to that." His mother ended the call.

Easton cleared his throat, all too aware of the possible bill that could come with the damage he'd caused to the vending machine. "Sorry about the mess. I can leave my credit card information with the supply manager if I need."

"I'm more interested in your hand." The doctor motioned to him. "And your arm."

"Oh, no. It's fine. Thanks. Just a few scrapes. Nothing I haven't survived before." Easton pocketed his phone. "You said Laila Ballard is stable. Can I talk to her?"

"Not yet. The patient didn't just manage to cut through her carotid artery. She pressed hard enough to damage her vocal cords. It'll be a few months before she can speak verbally," the physician said. "We've managed to stop the bleeding but she's still unconscious. I can let you know when she's out of surgery."

"Thanks." Easton couldn't fight back the memory of what'd happened in that room, of Laila Ballard blaming Genevieve for what'd happened with her daughter. The woman had enlisted the help of a serial killer to carry out her revenge. Which meant she had to have known about Lieutenant Parrish's dark side. But why kill him before the job was done? Staging her abduction, he could understand. Laila Ballard had needed a way to lure her target out of hiding, but if Genevieve was the endgame, why dispose of the man who'd done her dirty work until now? To give her the honor of finishing the job only to end her own life next? To tie up loose ends? Easton called after the doctor already heading back down the hall. "All updates on Laila Ballard are supposed to go through Captain Morsey. Have you tried getting a hold of him?"

"Captain Morsey isn't answering pages or his

phone," the attending said. "You may want to check with security."

"Will do. Thanks again." Easton followed the corridor past the waiting room and got the attention of an officer he recognized from Laila Ballard's crime scene. Hopefully there were no hard feelings about him lying to get past the perimeter tape. "Hey, man. I'm trying to track down Captain Morsey. Have you or your partner seen him around?"

"No. He radioed into dispatch about fifteen minutes ago, said he was end of watch." The officer accepted a cup of coffee from his partner and slugged it down. "After everything that happened today, I don't blame him. Parrish and the captain were close. Damn, I never would've pegged Parrish to be wrapped up in this. Abduction, killing. The guy was volunteering at La Puente every weekend. He'd pull over during shift to help folks get their groceries into their cars. Just doesn't make sense."

Alamosa PD had lost one of their own tonight, and the captain had gone home for the day? "Did Parrish and Laila Ballard know each other?"

"Nah, most of the time Ms. Ballard came around it was because she was looking for more information on her daughter's case." The second officer motioned toward Easton with his near-empty coffee cup. "She might've run into Parrish once in a while at the station, but Captain was the one who had her in his office week after week trying to keep her in the loop."

"Laila and the captain. Really? I didn't realize they knew each other." Easton tried to recall when Laila Ballard's daughter had been hit and killed by the drunk driver from Genevieve's prosecution record. Two years? Three? If their abduction victim was coming into the captain's office for weeks on end, they might've struck up a friendship. Maybe a deal? He'd talked to Captain Morsey on the way in. He'd been concerned about Laila, worried even, but the look in his eyes hadn't matched his expression. Easton had dismissed it as stress. Stress from a serial killer stringing up Alamosa residents, stress from discovering one of his own responsible, stress from shouldering the safety of this town. Fifteen minutes ago. The same time Genevieve had run out the side door… "Excuse me."

Easton followed the signs to the security office and requested access to the video feeds from the side door. Within a minute, he pegged Genevieve escaping into the parking lot, but seconds later, she disappeared off the screen. He pointed to the monitor. "Can you track her?"

The head of security accessed the second feed, one positioned over the emergency room entrance. There. Two police vehicles had been parked in the semicircle wrapping the front drive. Genevieve headed straight for the one on the left. The driver stepped out from behind the wheel. Captain Morsey. She collapsed into the passenger side. Easton pulled his phone free and dialed the number of her burner. "Come on, come on. Pick up, damn it."

The line went straight to voicemail.

Chapter Thirteen

"I guess the gig is up," he said.

She felt as though déjà vu was playing a cruel game with her head.

Shadows crept across the hardwood floor, just as they did the last night she'd walked into her home. Moonlight filtered through the sheer curtains. She could even still see the outline of blood the crime scene unit hadn't been able to get out of the wood. Her neck burned from the previous sting of the blade as she tried to work her tongue around the gag. The fabric wicked moisture from her lips and mouth, making it that much harder to swallow. Blood and pain and steel was all she knew now. She struggled against unconsciousness. Sweat slid down her face and into the collar of her blouse. Her head sagged forward, but he was there. He wouldn't let her sleep.

The installation of the first steel eyelet had kept her from fighting back as he'd drilled into the side of her knee. It didn't matter if she escaped now. She wouldn't be able to get far.

The man who'd haunted her nightmares sat himself on one of her barstools a few feet away. His fingers moved over the drill bit as he cleaned away her blood. She should've known. She should've known it'd been him that night. Barring her from the investigation, pressing her to admit she'd been the one to kill Elisa Johnson, blocking Battle Mountain PD from getting involved. Captain Morsey had been inside the investigation all along, leading it wherever he needed it to go. He'd known where to find her, that she'd borrowed a car from Laila Ballard and had a connection to each of the victims. He'd been the Contractor all along.

"You're a fighter, Counselor. I guessed as much. The way you make your case in court... So compelling." Morsey finished wiping the blood from his drill. The lamp in the corner glinted off the gold-colored metal bit. Shoving to his feet, he faced her. Ready to place the next piece of his sick puzzle. "Usually by this time, women your size need a little help staying awake, but I've always underestimated you, haven't I? I certainly did when I left you in the woods. Didn't think you'd last long enough for Ford to find you alive."

Easton. His name settled at the front of her mind and took up as much space as it could. Their last conversation threatened to break her all over again, but she had to stay strong. Mentally, physically, emotionally. She wasn't going to let Morsey win.

"Why?" The single word died at the gag squeezing her head. She pulled at the ties hinged inside the hooks he'd installed into her ceiling stretching her arms over her head. Her left toes barely skimmed the floor, an ache bunching along her sides. He'd planned to kill her in those woods. She had no doubt about that now as he slowly prepared to hang her from the ceiling, but he must've been interrupted. Maybe heard the sirens as Easton and the two Alamosa officers arrived at Parrish's cabin. He'd lost his opportunity.

"Every week for three years, Laila Ballard was waiting for me at the station. Every week I sat her down. I patted her shoulder. I listened to her when she could speak through the sobs." His gaze distanced as he adjusted his grip around the drill. "The law had failed her. You and everyone else involved in her daughter's case had failed her, and there was nothing I could do but watch this beautiful women break over and over again every week. I'm not sure when it happened, when I swore I would do whatever it took to ease her pain. She's a magnificent woman who didn't deserve what she went through. It was my job to fix it."

Her heart shuttered. Captain Morsey had fallen

in love with Laila Ballard. Over the course of those visits, he'd taken on the weight of her pain, her sorrow. He'd killed for her.

"By killing those women." Her lips barely met over the mouthful of the gag.

"To be honest, I wasn't sure I could do it." Morsey lowered the bright yellow power tool to his side, his aged index finger over the trigger. She'd managed to stay conscious through one eyelet in her joint. She wasn't sure she could through the second. "I had everything I needed. Profiles and surveillance on Elisa Johnson, Annette, Ruby Wagner and you. I learned your routines, tapped your phone lines, kept tabs on who you spoke to and cared about. I was ready to do this for Laila, but then Maria Gutierrez came along."

The hairs on the back of Genevieve's neck stood on end. The first victim. She pulled against the anchors he'd installed in her ceiling the night he'd killed Elisa Johnson, but they wouldn't budge. They'd held her assistant's weight for hours. They'd hold hers when he was finished with her. She rubbed the gag against her arm, dislodging it enough to breathe clearly for the first time in over an hour. "Maria wasn't a target."

Morsey stared down at the point where her toes skimmed the floor. Blood pooled beneath her, her slacks not thick enough to hold any more. "She was a good kid. I helped her apply to the Bureau, study for her exams. I gave her a reference and recommended for her to talk to some contacts I had."

"She must've seen something. Something she shouldn't have." Genevieve raised her gaze to the ceiling, all too aware Morsey held the upper hand here. She was hanging from the ceiling. The zip ties had cut into her wrists, and there was a steel eyelet screwed into her right knee. Still, there had to be something—anything—here that would help her get free.

"One night, Maria had come over to return one of my books. I invited her in out of habit. She saw the surveillance photos I'd taken of Annette Scofield on the table. I tried to tell her Scofield was the subject of an Internal Affairs investigation, but the look in her eyes… I could tell she didn't believe me." Morsey stepped into her, his dark eyes level with hers. He'd aged in a matter of hours. No longer the captain she'd worked with over the years, but someone she didn't recognize. "I didn't learn until later she'd called 9-1-1 when she got home that night, but accessing the recording—deleting it—would've raised too many flags. I had to wait so as not to spook her."

"You killed her to stop her from exposing you." Genevieve balled one fist and relaxed the muscles along her ribs as long as she could. One shot. That was all she had, but her toes barely swept across the hardwood. She wasn't strong enough to pull free.

She'd have to jump in to unhook the zip tie from the ceiling, and her knee had been taken out of commission. "Is that what happened to Lieutenant Parrish, too? He got too close? Is that why you framed him for abducting Laila?"

"Parrish should've left well enough alone." Morsey shook his head as though in regret. "I was careful, but he followed me after the news of Laila's disappearance hit the news. I led him straight to where she was hiding when I went to check on her. He must've seen Laila through the window. I went to refresh her supplies, and he broke in, thinking I was holding her hostage. Laila had no choice but to kill him. He would've ruined everything."

"She cut off her own ear to lure me to the house." Genevieve's toes pressed into the hardwood. The muscles along her sides were lengthening with every exhale. "Why the pageantry? Why hang them from their ceilings? Why all of this?"

Sweat trickled into her eye and down her throat. Blood loss raised her pulse. Her nerves worked overtime to compensate for the pain in her knee, but there was only so much her body could do. Spidery lines crept into the edges of her vision.

"I wasn't going to let anything link back to Laila. If I made it look like a serial killer was on the loose, I could hide the connection between the victims. It worked for a while. Until you and Easton Ford insisted on getting involved." Morsey crouched, gripping her leg below her left knee. He stared up at her and pressed the drill bit into her. "Sorry, kid. I made a deal, and I'm a man of my word." He lifted the drill parallel to the floor.

No. This wasn't over. She wasn't going to die like this. "He won't stop. Easton will figure it out. He'll come for you, and you and Laila will never get to be together." It was the only play she had left. "That's what you want, isn't it? You love her. You killed for her. You can still walk away. You can disappear, but only if I make it out of this alive."

Her heart jerked in her chest at the thought of never seeing Easton Ford again. Those sea-blue eyes lighting up whenever she walked into the room, that smile that swept away violence and fear and loneliness. He'd always had that effect on her, as though he'd always been right there in the back of her mind. She'd battled long and hard for her independence, to prove she was more than his girl, his fiancée. His. But now… Now she understood. He hadn't just been at the back of her mind. He'd become part of her. He was hers, and no matter how many times she'd tried to deny it, she'd fallen in love with him all over again. Her friend, her protector, her everything. Hers.

Hesitation lightened the pressure of the drill bit against her knee. Captain Morsey's eyes grew dazed, but not long enough. He readjusted his grip on the drill and leveled it off again. "It's too late for that."

"No!" Genevieve ripped her leg out of his clutch and jumped as high as she could. Her descending tug snapped the zip tie around her left wrist, and she swung off-center. Kicking out, she kicked Morsey back, but the pain in her right knee kept her from making contact with the floor. She was still hanging from the ceiling by one arm, and the tie sliced deeper. Blood slid down her forearm as her attacker regained his footing. A scream tore from her throat as she stretched her right toes for the edge of the brick fireplace, but she couldn't lift herself higher to break the second zip tie.

Morsey shot his hand out, securing her throat in a strong grip, and pulled her into him. "You're going to regret that."

THEY'D HAD THE wrong man.

Captain Morsey was the one who'd had a personal relationship with Laila Ballard. Not Parrish. He had a knowledge of forensics, access to each of the victims, inside information concerning the investigation—it all added up. He was the killer. He was behind this entire mind game.

Easton fled out the front emergency room doors, both officers on his heels. He had to think. Morsey couldn't have taken her far. Killers stuck to their hunting grounds unless forced to break habit. He ran through the parameters Weston had set from the beginning. Isolated, quiet, guarded. Morsey wouldn't go back to Parrish's cabin or the scene where Laila Ballard had been reportedly held. They were still crime scenes. "Damn it. He could be anywhere."

"Captain still isn't answering his phone," one of the officers reported. "Laila Ballard accused Lieutenant Parrish of abducting her. Now you think it's the captain? You've got a lot of nerve, Ford. Captain's a good man. He wouldn't do anything like this."

His exhales crystalized in front of his mouth. The spike in his heart rate beaded sweat in his hairline. The ringing started in his ears, too loud. Hell, he didn't have time for this. Genevieve didn't have time for this. He had to slow down, had to think. "Parrish must've gotten too close. He became a loose end. Laila killed him to keep us from exposing the truth. She's been working with Captain Morsey all along."

Genevieve. He closed his eyes against the oncoming attack of personal failures, but…they never came. The ringing blended in with the white noise of traffic outside the hospital's front doors. His pulse thudded hard behind his ears. He forced himself to take a deep breath and focus on nothing but her until the dull piercing in his ears vanished altogether. His senses evened out. He could do this. He could save her.

"Morsey took advantage when Genevieve came

around that corner." Easton pointed back to the southeast corner of the building, where surveillance had lost her. "He'd come to the hospital because he'd heard what'd happened to Laila, but he couldn't pass up the opportunity to finish what he started. Not when she was too emotionally compromised to see him for who he really was. Laila was supposed to be the one to kill Genevieve, but she tried to take her own life instead. He wasn't prepared to abduct her, which means he didn't have a location set up to finish the job. If he wants to stick to his MO, he'll have to take her somewhere familiar. Somewhere he's already set up."

"You mean one of the crime scenes where the victims were found hanging from the ceilings," the second officer said. "They've all been processed by CSU. Everything the killer used at those scenes is in evidence."

Easton turned on them, his head clearer than it had been in months. "What about Genevieve Alexander's home? It hasn't officially been released by the crime scene techs. Have any officers been posted for security since Laila Ballard was taken?"

Shock filtered across the first uniform's expression. He looked to his partner. "Captain Morsey pulled uniforms off security once Ms. Ballard was reported missing. He wanted all available units working her abduction."

"Leaving the scene unsecure." Easton clenched his fist around his keys. "That's where he's taken her. We need to get over there now."

Neither officer argued this time as they ran to their cruiser. Easton sprinted across the parking lot and shoved his key in the old worn lock of his pickup, nearly breaking it in half in the process. He slid behind the peeling leather steering wheel and started the engine. The truck coughed, violent and exhausted, but he couldn't wait for it to warm up. Shoving it into gear, he fishtailed out of the parking lot.

A coat slid across the passenger seat at a hard right turn and bundled against his leg. Genevieve's. She'd been in such a rush to talk to Laila in the hospital, she must've left it behind. His lungs gave under the pressure of holding his breath. Their last conversation edged into his consciousness as the small town blurred through the windows. As much as it'd hurt to watch her walk out that door, she was right. All these years he'd tried fitting her into this…mold he'd needed in his life. A release, an emotional regulator, a lover, a listener, a companion. She was supposed to be the answer to his pain when he should've been the one to confront it head on, to take responsibility. Not hiding in the middle of his family's property, chasing away the only people willing to give him the time of day. The protest of leather in his hand kept him anchored into the moment, focused. Hell, she wasn't accountable for the hollowness in his chest, but he'd put the expectation on her to heal him anyway. No. The trauma he'd survived, the mental side effects of war and loss and grief, that was on him. How hadn't he been able to see it before now?

The answer was already there. Because he hadn't wanted to. Because it'd been easier to blame outside forces than to face his failure. But the truth was there, buried, but there. He hadn't seen her as anything more than someone to protect in that cafeteria back in high school, or his girlfriend when they'd started dating. His fiancée when he'd slid that ring onto her finger. The truth was, keeping his eyes on the road during his last supply run wouldn't have stopped that IED from taking out his unit. The truth was, his father had sacrificed himself doing the very thing he'd instilled in both of his sons, the ultimate example of selflessness and love.

He loved Genevieve. More than he'd loved anyone else in his life, but he'd been selfish since the moment she'd knocked on his door three days ago. In reality, he hadn't given her any other choice but to walk away. She'd held true to herself, and he'd discarded her for his own hubris.

Easton maneuvered onto her street and slammed on the brakes in front of her house. The rambler-style structure had been well-kept, the lawn perfectly manicured and welcoming. Genevieve hadn't just escaped to Alamosa. She'd made a career here, friends, a home. He didn't have any right to take that from her, even in the name of love.

He released his grip on the steering wheel as the Alamosa patrol cruiser pulled up behind him. This was it. The endgame.

The two officers from the hospital hit the sidewalk, each armed. The one closest to him nodded. "You strapped?"

"No." He'd sworn never to handle a firearm since his discharge with one exception: the night of his father's death. Adrenaline curled his fingers into fists as the second officer handed off a backup piece. He released the magazine, counted the rounds, and slammed it back into place before loading a bullet in the chamber. He faced the house, every muscle down his spine tightening with battle-ready tension. "Let's go."

Keeping low, they approached in a triangular formation. Easton signaled one officer off to the left, around the back, and for the other to stick with him. No sign of the captain's patrol vehicle parked out front or along the block, but that didn't mean the bastard hadn't stashed it out of sight.

He kept an eye on the windows for any sign of movement, but the night held still. Taking position on one side of the front door, he waited as the Alamosa officer took the other. He'd trained for this. He was good at this. He wouldn't fail Genevieve again.

Easton nodded then tested the doorknob.

It turned easily in his hand, and the painted wood swung inward.

Shadows cut across the hardwood floor. He'd studied the crime scene photos of Elisa Johnson's murder, but he hadn't realized how…normal the house itself was. A woven rug led them deeper into the home before the space opened into the front living room where Genevieve had discovered the body of her assistant. Comfortable sofas and a warm wood coffee table had been positioned for conversation while the massive stone fireplace—most likely original to the home—demanded attention. Obvious care and an immaculate setting of decor might've lured him into a false sense of security if he hadn't noticed the corner of the hearth was missing. He stepped into the living room, his gaze automatically seeking the hooks the killer would've installed to hang Elisa Johnson from the ceiling.

They were still there, but there was no sign of Genevieve.

Where else would Morsey have taken her? All of the other crime scenes had been released, his equipment logged into evidence. No. She had to be here. Easton twisted, his boot nearly slipping out from underneath him. He caught himself on the stone mantel. Blood. It'd almost blended in with the color of the dark wood, but there was no mistaking it now. It hadn't dried, and CSU wouldn't have left it behind, which meant... His grip slipped against the steel of his flashlight, and the resulting wound from his confrontation with Laila Ballard and the lacerations across his knuckles flared. "Genevieve."

"Clear!" The officers hadn't found anyone else in the house.

Easton studied the room before moving on to the kitchen then the guest bedroom and Genevieve's bedroom. A sleek black-and-white box stared back at him from the nightstand beside her bed. Chocolates. Where was she? He leveraged his weight against the door frame of her bedroom. The house was empty, and from the amount of blood he'd stepped in, Genevieve was running out of time. She'd been injured, but he had to believe Morsey would keep to his MO. All of the other victims had been kept conscious while he'd strung them up. It would've taken hours depending on how hard the women had struggled. Genevieve was a fighter. She wouldn't give up, and neither would he.

He stepped back into the hallway. If Genevieve had been moved as the evidence suggested, there had to be a trail. He retraced his steps back to the front room. "There's a fresh pool of blood by the fireplace. He must've moved her. Look for blood evidence. I need to know where he took her." If Morsey had moved her in a state of panic, the captain wouldn't have had time to clean up his mess. Both officers separated as Easton studied his own bloody footprints on the hardwood. He'd compromised the scene in his search, but he couldn't worry about that right now. He heel-toed it slowly across the floor, each board vibrating under his weight, then froze. He stomped his foot harder and honed his flashlight beam on the floor.

He'd repaired enough floorboards over the years to know the sound difference between a foundation and a basement. Whispering Pines cabins didn't have basements. The reverberation under his foot here, however, was deeper, longer. He whistled as softly as he could manage, the same whistle that'd always let his family know where he was when they'd gone out hunting.

The Alamosa officers converged, following his motion as he pointed to the floor.

Easton nodded. "She's in the basement."

Chapter Fourteen

Footsteps shook dust loose from the subfloor above her.

It filtered down through the light given off by the bare bulb, but she couldn't call out, couldn't scream. The pain and blood loss from the injury to her knees had stolen her voice. She tried to lift her head away from her chest, but the gravity on her skull was too much to fight. She had to stay awake, had to warn whoever was searching the house. She couldn't see Morsey anymore. He'd slipped into the shadows with a finger pressed to his mouth and the drill in his hand.

Genevieve tried to turn her wrist under the layered wrap of fishing line, but the chair he'd tied her to wouldn't budge under pressure. Not that she had much left to give anyway. A small whimper escaped up her throat. The gag had soaked through. Same as her clothing. Sweat, blood, tears—it all mixed to add to the weight on her body. Her spine stretched long. She'd managed to free herself from one hook upstairs, but it hadn't been enough. Morsey had ensured she'd never be able to walk again when he'd drilled the second eyelet into her opposite knee.

Silence burned in her ears.

No more footsteps. No more voices. No more help.

A deep sob replaced her low whimper. No one was coming for her.

Bare cement walls absorbed the frigidness of spring and filled the space with a chill. Her skin contracted in response. Insulation glittered under the exposed bulb from between bare-minimum framing. Cracks spread across the cement from the corners of the main room and branched off out of sight. The builder had wanted an arm and a leg to finish the space. Money she hadn't been able to afford at the time. Maybe that was a good thing. It was hard to get blood out of carpet and drywall. She'd never liked the basement in this house, using it for nothing more than Christmas decoration storage. Now she would die here.

The thought wedged through the lightheadedness. She didn't want to die. She'd worked too hard for the life she'd built. She'd survived loneliness and shame and self-consciousness and heartbreak, and she wasn't ready to stop feeling. She wanted to live, to love, to laugh. Nothing else mattered. She wanted Easton, and there was no way in hell she was going to give up now.

The layout of this floor mimicked the one above, only there were very few walls separating her from the stairs. Fifteen hundred square feet of inky blackness and angles she couldn't see around. Morsey would see her given the right angle. She had to move fast. She tugged against the fishing line. Blood bloomed in thin rivulets across her wrist. Rolling her head to one side, she struggled to catch something—anything—to give her an idea of where her killer had gone. Nothing. She'd wasted enough time walking through life afraid. It was time to take control. Genevieve pressed her teeth together as she strained against the fishing line. Pain exploded up her arm, but she couldn't stop. The groan lodged in her throat escaped as her skin broke under the pressure.

The fishing line snapped.

Momentum shot her arm up and tipped the chair to one side. Oxygen caught in her chest as the world threatened to rip straight out from under her, but she found balance. Scanning the shadows, she waited. Waited for Morsey to stop her, to end the insufferable pain in her knees. There was only silence. Genevieve threaded her fingers under the line securing her opposite arm to the chair and pulled as hard as she could. The second line broke with a soft split, and she unwound it slowly from around her wrist. Morsey hadn't taken the time to secure her legs. There'd been no need with the damage done. She was free.

Using the chair arms as leverage, she gritted against the agony ripping through her knees and slid to the glacial cement floor. Dust clung to her palms and clothing as she rolled onto her front. The eyelets Morsey had drilled into the outer edges of her knees brushed against the floor as she attempted to push off with her toes, and Genevieve slammed her hand against the floor to stay conscious. Lightning struck behind her eyes. She forced herself to keep breathing, to stay in the moment. She had to move, but the harder she pushed herself, the faster she'd bleed out.

The window behind her. It was the only escape Morsey couldn't cover if he was ensuring no one would interrupt him by the stairs. Or was this part of the game? Make her think she had a chance only to violently rip it away from her in the end? She didn't want to believe the captain she'd trusted had fallen prey to that evil part of him that'd given him the ability to kill innocent women, but maybe it was too late. The drowning pull of blood loss thickened, but she couldn't stop. Not yet. She set her weight in her elbows and dragged herself away from the chair. The eyelets scraped against the floor, too loud in her ears, but moving slower only increased her chances of getting caught all over again. Her muscles ached. It was getting harder to breathe, to keep her eyes open.

The light cut out, throwing her into utter darkness.

Her breath sawed in and out of her throat. She hadn't heard him enter the room. He couldn't have cut the power, which meant... Whoever'd been upstairs. They were still here. Tears of relief burned, but she couldn't relax yet. As long as Morsey held on to his power over her, she was still trapped. The only advantage she had was knowing the exact layout of her own house. The captain might be able to move faster, but he was in unfamiliar territory.

"Genevieve…" His voice pierced through the dizzying layer of fear gripping the muscles down her legs in remembered agony. The high-pitched whine of the drill filled her ears. "I can hear you breathing. You can't hide from me."

She forced herself to hold her breath. She stretched her palms out in front of her, searching for something to use as a weapon. She hadn't been down here in months. She'd had no reason, but she wished she'd hidden an additional firearm down here as well as in her fireplace upstairs. The window couldn't be more than a few feet away, but at the same time it felt as though it were another mile ahead of her. Where were the people she'd heard upstairs? Had they given up? Had Morsey used his charm and authority to convince them there was nothing wrong? Genevieve forced herself to still, to buy herself more time.

No one was coming to save her.

She had to save herself.

Her fingers brushed over one of the larger cracks in the concrete from the house settling over the years. Movement registered a few feet off to her left, and she jammed her nails inside the small crack. She worked as fast as possible while trying not to give away her position in the dark. Morsey had been relying on her house electricity to keep the upper hand. He hadn't brought a flashlight or emergency supplies. Now she had the advantage.

"You can't escape, Genevieve. Those eyelets in your knees? It'll be impossible to walk, let alone run from me." His voice moved with him, farther away, possibly facing the opposite direction. "Even if you manage to get out of here, I'll find you. There's nowhere you can go I won't follow. One way or another, I'm going to keep my end of the deal I made with Laila. I'm not leaving until you pay for failing her."

A sliver of concert broke off in her hand. Genevieve slowed, waiting. She pressed the edge of the shard into her palm. It wasn't much. It might not hold up against an attack, but she would do whatever it took to get out of this basement alive. Moving slower than she wanted to go, she swept her legs out to the side and balanced on one hip.

There was no making it to the window now. Not without drawing his attention. Who knew when the power might come back on. She had to make herself as small a target as possible until then, had to hide. The Christmas decorations. She'd stacked the boxes in the corner of this main room. There could be space behind the one she'd stored her tree in. A few seconds. That was all she needed. It might be enough until help arrived.

Easton would find her. She had to believe that. No matter how many times she'd hurt him, how strained their relationship, she'd always been able to count on him. He'd come through this time, too. He'd know she'd been taken. He'd figure out by who and where Morsey had brought her. He'd finish what they'd started and bring justice to the women Genevieve hadn't been able to protect.

Her hands shook as she rose to sit on her bottom. The concrete shard cut into her hand, but it was nothing compared to the agony burning through her knees. She set her weight into the base of her palms and tugged herself in the direction she believed the boxes would be. Her bare heels dragged against the cold floor, a whimper in the blackness.

"Marco…" The sound of the drill ticked off in rhythm to her racing heartbeat. Followed by three heavy footsteps. His boots scraped across the floor, accentuated by the layer of dust that'd accumulated over the years. "That's when you say Polo, Genevieve. Come on, play the game with me. Don't let the last moments of your life be made up of nothing but pain and desperation. Marco…"

She kept moving. She shot her hand out to get a feel for how far away she was from the boxes but met nothing but air. Ice infused her veins. She was still in the middle of the room, still exposed. Gravity and blood loss pulled her to the floor.

The single bare bulb in the room brightened.

Genevieve froze.

Morsey turned. He took a single step forward, his mouth stretching into an uneven smile as he advanced.

Another outline penetrated her peripheral vision as Easton raised his weapon. "Polo."

HIS GUN WARMED in his grip. It'd been months since he'd held a firearm, let alone pulled the trigger, but muscle memory had him taking aim between Morsey's eyes. "Put the weapon down, turn your back to me and interlace your hands behind your head. Now."

"She doesn't have much time, Ford." Morsey bent at the knees to set down the drill with one hand, the other raised in surrender. "Are you sure you want to waste the precious minutes you have left together on me?"

The only dry-walled wall framing the stairs blocked his view of Genevieve on the other side of the room. All he saw was blood. A long trail soaked into the concrete stretching the length of half the room, and his imagination was all too willing to fill in the blanks. Easton's mouth dried as he forced himself to step completely in the room. Genevieve.

The source of the blood seemed to be coming from both of her knees where Morsey had screwed in the same type of steel eyelets he'd used on his previous victims. The captain had been getting ready to hang her from the ceiling. Just like all the others. "You son of a bitch."

"Let's leave the name calling at the door, Ford." Morsey lowered his hands to his sides. "You knew exactly what you were getting yourself into when you decided to intervene in my investigation. Now, you've got a choice to make. Save Ms. Alexander or take me into custody."

Numbness spread from his fingers down his arms as the seconds distorted into minutes. He moved deeper into the room. He studied her, unconscious, bleeding out, and his entire world shattered in the span of a single exhale. One moment, he was standing in the center of Genevieve's basement, and the next he'd been right back in that wreckage. Struggling to pull his unit from the carnage and flames.

"Time's up, Ford." Morsey lunged. The captain slammed his hand into Easton's forearm, and the gun slipped from his grasp. A solid kick crushed the air from his lungs, and Easton fell back. Morsey stood over him, fisting one hand in Easton's collar, and pulled his elbow back. The right hook shot Easton's head back into the concrete, followed quickly by Morsey's left. "You can't stop me."

The Afghanistan sun superimposed the bare light bulb above then flickered back. Morsey himself dissolved into a soldier who'd caught up with the convoy, yelling at him through the ringing in his ears. Another strike from Morsey's left fist craned his head to one side, toward Genevieve. Her delicate features blended with those of Ripper's as the only female in his unit lay dead on the cracked asphalt. His heart thudded hard behind his ears. Hot sand and cold concrete twisted in an alternate reality he wasn't sure he could differentiate.

Morsey pulled him from the floor, the captain's outline blurring in front of him. "You can't help her, Ford. You can't even help yourself."

Easton blinked against the lightning streaking across his vision. Morsey was right. He couldn't help Genevieve. He couldn't help anyone. Not like this. Not with the past suffocating him from the inside. Not with pain and grief holding him back from moving on with his life. A glimmer of life opened Genevieve's eyes a fraction of an inch, and the buzz in his head quieted. For the first time in years, the hollowness in his chest didn't hurt. Because of her.

Morsey pulled back to strike again.

Easton caught the captain's fist in his palm. He clenched the killer's shirt in his other and slammed his head into Morsey's. The police captain fell back.

Blood spewed down the man's face as Easton pushed to his feet. "She's not yours to claim, Morsey."

He launched his right hook straight into the bastard's temple. Pain rocketed down his hand and into his elbow, but he couldn't stop. He kicked Morsey's knee out from the back and forced the killer down.

The flash of metal was all the warning he got as the captain swung up. The blade hit into Easton's side. Pain arched through him, and Easton stumbled back into the nearest wall, holding his side. Morsey struggled for breath as he hauled himself to his feet. "Didn't that brother of yours teach you to always carry a backup weapon, Ford?"

"Didn't they teach you to always wear your body armor in the academy?" He straightened. Movement registered from behind the killer, and Easton straightened. It was over. The bastard who'd ripped his world in two had nowhere to go. He nodded over Morsey's shoulder. "Besides, why would I need a backup weapon when I have her?"

The captain turned to confront the threat, but he wasn't fast enough.

Two gunshots exploded in the small space as Genevieve pulled the trigger.

Morsey arched against the impact, eyes wide, jowls frozen with surprised creases. The killer dropped harder than the box of rocks Easton used to collect under his bed as a kid.

The thud of metal against concrete shot Easton forward. Genevieve collapsed onto her back, her eyes rolling up into her head. The gun slipped from her grasp as he threaded one hand behind her neck. "Stay with me, Genevieve. You're not allowed to die now."

No response.

Footsteps raced down the stairs. He'd left both Alamosa officers to wait for the ambulance, but they wouldn't have been able to ignore two gunshots. Identifying shouts pierced the high-pitched ringing in his ears from the shots as the officers rounded into the room, weapons up and aimed. Hesitation filtered across their expressions as they took in the scene. Their captain on the floor, the drill near the body, the bloody trail leading to Genevieve and the weapon beside her. It all added up.

But Easton didn't have time to catch them up. "Where the hell is that ambulance?"

"It just pulled up," one of the officers said. Another rumble of panicked footsteps bounced off the unfinished basement stairs. A pair of EMTs shoved both officers out of the way. One split toward the captain, the other toward Genevieve.

Easton's grip lightened on her as the EMT crouched to assess the damage. "Caucasian female, thirty-four years old, severe blood loss from the injuries in both knees."

"How long has she been unconscious?" The EMT

set a stethoscope in his ears and listened for Genevieve's pulse. Tugging it down around his neck, he wrapped a blood pressure cuff around her arm then got to work on an IV.

"About a minute, maybe a little longer." The time that'd distorted a few minutes ago seemed to catch up with him all at once. Easton scrubbed a hand down his face, the other interlaced in Genevieve's. Her fingers were cold. She'd lost too much blood in too short of a time. "I'm not sure how much blood she's lost. There's what's down here and a puddle upstairs in the living room."

"The captain's dead on arrival over here. Detectives will be notified." The second EMT maneuvered to Genevieve's head and took over assessing her vital signs. "Sir, we need you to back away. Let us do our jobs."

"Please. Save her." He'd never been so desperate in his life. Shoving to his feet, Easton stumbled back against a collection of boxes packed with glittery balls and brightly colored ribbon. Christmas decorations. The cardboard nearly gave way under his weight, but he only had attention for Genevieve. For the perfect curve of her upper lip, the beauty mark he'd memorized so many times, the angle of her delicate jawline. She'd shared the greatest gift she ever could've given him during this investigation: healing. Now that gift would be taken from him.

"We're going to do everything in our power, sir, but we can't stop the bleeding until we get those screws out of her knees. We've got to move." Faster than he thought possible, EMTs hauled Genevieve onto a stretcher and had secured her for transport. They wound through the sharp angles of the basement layout and up the stairs. The oxygen mask placed over her mouth and nose cut off his view of most of her face. She'd survived the Contractor. That was all that mattered.

Police sirens and red and blue patrol lights converged outside the house as Easton followed emergency personnel out the front door. Alamosa PD officers sprinted past him, presumably at the call of their fellow brothers in blue still assessing the scene downstairs. EMTs loaded Genevieve into the back of the ambulance. The urge to climb in right behind her, to hold her hand in case she woke up midtransport to the hospital raged hard.

"Easton!" His brother's voice drowned out the controlled chaos around him. An officer tried to stop Weston from entering the scene as the crime scene tape was going up, but he flashed his badge with a don't-mess-with-me expression. "Considering your captain is the one behind these deaths, I recommend you let me by, Officer. You're going to need me."

Easton couldn't move, couldn't think. His gaze drifted back to the ambulance as the rig's sirens first chirped then screeched through the lightening morning. It pulled away from the curb and disappeared around the corner. Before he had a chance to make sense of what'd happened, Genevieve was gone.

"You've got blood on you." Weston settled dark brown eyes on him—the same color as their dad's—and fisted one sleeve of Easton's shirt. His brother scanned him from head to toe, presumably looking for an injury, but he wouldn't find any. Not any he could see anyway.

The pulsing in his ears intensified the longer he stood there. He licked dry lips, caught in the middle of considering climbing into his truck or staying to give his statement and help with the scene. Alamosa PD was hurting right now. Their lieutenant had been framed and murdered, and their captain had been behind a handful of murders in the name of love. They needed him. "It's not mine."

"Easton." Weston shook his arm, forcing him back into the moment. Understanding smoothed the harsh lines around his brother's mouth, the past couple years more evident in the creases around his eyes and mouth. But there was a warmth Easton hadn't seen since Weston had lost his wife all those years ago. Something that had to do with Chloe. "Go." His brother slapped him on the back. "You're no good here like this. Go. I've got this handled."

Easton ran toward the truck and his future.

Chapter Fifteen

She was tired of hospitals.

Tired of the incessant beeping of the monitors, of the dull ache in her knees not even pain medication could touch. Tired of the images her mind insisted on processing over and over when she closed her eyes. She'd lived through the worst trauma of her life, but had she survived? Captain Morsey had taken so many lives. Hers would be another tally on his belt.

The hospital room door clicked open, but she didn't have the inclination to greet one of the many doctors and nurses who'd bustled in and out of here. The surgeons had done what they could to repair the tears in her knees, but there would be permanent damage. The drill had severed the lateral collateral ligament on the outer sides of her knees. A complete separation. In a matter of minutes, Captain Morsey had ripped away her ability to walk away from this on her own two feet.

The wheelchair her physicians had showed her how to use earlier sat off to her right. Tears burned as she studied the black leather and chrome handles. Rawness scratched up her throat from her previous encounter with Morsey out at the dunes. "I'm too broke to buy anything, I know who I'm voting for and I've found Jesus. Unless you're here with a giant box of chocolate or another dose of morphine, I'm not interested."

"Then this is your lucky day." That voice. His voice. She'd dreamed about it while under the sedatives. It'd been the last thing she'd heard in that basement, and the first thing she'd craved when she'd woken up in this room, but he hadn't been here. "One giant box of chocolates for you, Counselor." Easton flashed that charming smile that'd forced her insides into a riot as he set down a sleek black-and-white box with the manufacturer's name standing out in the corner. Thirty-six pieces of Belgian chocolate truffles created to look like jewels of the most expensive kind. "These ones don't have any eggs, marshmallow or graham cracker in them. I checked."

She didn't understand. "How did you—"

"I noticed a box on your nightstand in your bedroom during our search of your house." His smile slipped, and she was thrown back into harsh reality instead of the few seconds of safety she'd found in their conversation. Bandages hid an array of injuries across his hand and up his forearm.

He'd been there. He'd been one of the officers she'd heard on the main level after Morsey had moved her to the basement. He'd come for her. Genevieve set the square box on her lap but didn't move to open it. "You knew he would bring me back there. Even after I told you I didn't want there to be more between us, you came for me."

"I wasn't going to let him hurt you, Genevieve." Those sea-blue eyes she'd equated with the loss of her identity studied the bulbous bandages wrapped around her knees beneath the thin sheets. "I'm sorry I wasn't fast enough."

Phantom pain prickled down her shins. After what they'd been through together, she didn't have much of a guard left anymore. "I'm in this bed recovering from surgery instead of lying to rest in the Alamosa Cemetery. This…didn't end like I thought it would, but I still owe you my life. I was hoping you'd be here when I woke up."

Easton hung his head, nodding only slightly. "I tried to be here when I heard you were out of surgery, but they wouldn't let me in the room. I may have made some threats after that. The administrators had one of their security guards sit with me until your doctors gave the okay for visitors once Weston vouched for me."

"Well, I appreciate the effort, and the chocolates. If you were hoping I'd share, you've got another thing coming." The bottom half of the box unsuctioned from the top, revealing a brightly colored array of gourmet chocolates. She chose a chocolate-and-pink-striped square of flavor and melted goodness and took a bite. Strawberry and dark cocoa burst across her tongue, urging her to forget everything that'd happened after the moment she'd knocked on Easton Ford's door. The bandages on her wrists punctuated how close she'd come to dying in her own house. Because despite the years she'd spent there, it could never be a home. Not anymore. "How is Laila Ballard doing?"

"She's alive, which is more than I can say for her partner. She'll spend the next few weeks recovering here, but once she's stable, your office will have Alamosa PD's full support in filing charges." He seemed to memorize the arrangement of truffles on her lap. Setting one hand against the guardrail alongside her bed, he tapped it with the base of his palm. Bruises darkened the circles under his eyes and marred the once perfect skin of his cheek. "She convinced Captain Morsey to kill those women, Genevieve. At the very least, she's looking at conspiracy to commit murder. She belongs behind bars."

"You think she's a monster." Genevieve handed off one of her favorites from the box.

"No, I think she's hurting." He bit into the circular truffle, chewing as though relishing every bite, and she didn't have the strength to look away. "But until she's ready to face that pain, she's going to keep hurting herself and others. Intentionally or not."

Genevieve set down the strawberry and chocolate combination. Her appetite for decadence vanished. The investigation, their interactions—they'd been playing in her mind since the moment she'd woken from surgery, and her insides somersaulted. "Before, when we were in the waiting room, you said you knew exactly what Laila Ballard went through. That your anger and betrayal made you run from the people who care about you, and you were on the same path as she was. What changed?"

"I had you." He said it so matter-of-factly, it was impossible to deny. Easton popped the rest of the truffle in his mouth. "As much as I blamed you for starting this…chain reaction in my life, you're the one who helped me see what was important. Showed me what I wanted and what I need to do to get better."

"What is it you want?" A tremor worked through her hands as she slipped them beneath her thighs. The movement caught his attention, and a rush of emotion lodged in her throat. Her nerves caught fire as he reached down and tugged one hand free, encasing it in both of his.

"You, Genevieve." Calluses scraped against her knuckles and heightened her senses into overdrive. "No matter how much time you want, how much space you need to figure out you and your independence, I'll wait. I'm in no rush."

Genevieve thwarted her expression's automatic response to contort into ugly-crying-face and set her free hand over his. "I want you, too. What I said before, about not wanting to get wrapped up in you and your personality and your family again—I didn't understand it at the time. You've been part of my life since I was sixteen. You've been a part of me since the moment you stood up for me in that cafeteria. If I lose you, I'll lose a piece of myself, and we've been apart long enough. I love you."

"I love you." Easton slipped his hands on either side of her face, careful of the bruises along her neck, and bent down. He pressed his mouth to hers, combining the aftertaste of his truffle mint with the strawberry still clinging to her tongue. The flavors danced alongside one another as he explored her mouth second by agonizing second. By the time he pulled away, she had a hard time remembering which chocolate she'd eaten and which one he'd finished. "Not sure I've ever mixed mint with strawberry." He swiped his thumb along the corner of his mouth. "I like it."

Her laugh shuddered through her, igniting another

ache along the outer edges of her knees. She rolled her lips between her teeth and bit down to give her brain something else to focus on, but she couldn't ignore the truth. "It's not going to be the same, is it?"

"No." Easton interlaced his fingers with hers. "It won't, but I'm going to be there every step of the way. Follow-up appointments, physical therapy, the nightmares. Whatever happens, we'll get through it. Together. Here in Alamosa or back in Battle Mountain. Wherever you need me, I'll be there."

She pressed her palms into the tops of her thighs, but the pain medication had taken away even the sense of pressure. Why then did she still feel the weight of what Morsey had done to her? "I can't go back to that house. Every time I think about finding Elisa in the living room, what he was going to do to me…" She closed her eyes.

"Hey, look at me. You don't have to." He notched her chin higher with one finger. Easton unlatched the guardrail and lowered it. Maneuvering onto the edge of the bed, he leveled her gaze with his. "You know that. We can find you a new place. You could come stay with me until you get settled."

"That cabin can barely hold my investigative files." She pressed her free hand to her forehead. "How are we going to make that work with two of us and my wheelchair in there? What about the commute?"

"We can find a place of our own," he said. "Here."

What? No. He'd already done so much for her, she couldn't ask for more. "Easton, I love my job. I ran for district attorney because I believed I could make a difference. I don't want to give that up, but I don't want you to have to give up the town you've felt safe in your whole life."

"I feel safe when I'm with you." Tucking his knuckle under her chin, he smiled. "If that means we're here in Alamosa and I'm not a Battle Mountain reserve officer anymore, so be it. I lost you once, Genevieve. I'm not willing to go through that again. Besides, there are more psychologists here who deal with PTSD."

Her heart squeezed in her chest, and she fell a little bit more in love with him right then. "Are you sure about this?"

"Who knows? Maybe Alamosa will be looking for a new officer given how they just lost two of their own." Easton eyed another one of her chocolates.

Her mouth stretched wide enough to tug on the split in her bottom lip, but she didn't care. Leaning in close, she kissed him, happier than she'd been in years. "I do like a man in uniform."

Three months later

WIND CUT THROUGH the pines around the cabin as he rounded the hood of the new truck. It wasn't anything he would've picked out for himself. Newer, less history, but it was perfect for allowing Genevieve to get in and out of easily and spacious enough to store her wheelchair in the back. He hauled the chair out of the truck bed and set it up a few feet away. Easton popped the passenger side door open and offered his hand.

Smooth skin brushed against calluses as Genevieve secured her hand in his. She maneuvered to the edge of the seat, her legs hanging over the side. Black leggings hid the scars originating around her knees and spreading up her thigh and down her shin on either side. The surgeries had gone as well as they ever could, but rehab was an entirely different beast altogether. Notwithstanding the immediate dive into physical therapy a day after her surgeries and her continued fight to make it through her exercises every day afterward, there were still no signs Genevieve would ever be able to walk on her own. She slid her arm over his shoulders as he positioned his under her knees. Just as they'd done a hundred times. "If this keeps up, you won't have to ever go back to the gym."

"One of the benefits of you not being able to run away." He set her in her seat and kicked down the footrests. Easton stepped to the back of the wheelchair and closed her passenger door before pushing her toward the main cabin.

Her smile overwhelmed the summer sun high overhead. She reached one hand back over her shoulder and settled it on top of his. "And the others?"

"We'll talk about those at home." Home. It'd had a different meaning up until Genevieve's discharge from the hospital. Whispering Pines had been the only place he'd found shelter from the world when it'd stopped making sense. Now he and Genevieve had a new place of their own. He, Weston and his mother had retrofitted the single-level house in Alamosa with wider doorways, a ramp leading up to the front door and even a massive tile shower large enough to fit her chair. It was perfect, but they made it a point to travel the three hours back here as often as possible. For his mom's sake. And his.

Karie Ford descended the main cabin's front steps, blocking the sun from her eyes. Her signature flannel shirt flapped with the breeze as she smiled at their approach. The new ramp addition to the cabin bled into the original design with dark wood and bright green trim, but that wasn't why he'd brought Genevieve here today. "Hey, you two. Hope you're hungry. Weston and Chloe might've eaten everything by now though."

Easton slowed, giving his mother a side hug. "Hey, Mom. The ramp looks great."

"Glad you like it. Felt good to keep my hands busy," Karie said. "Figured I can start making a few more adjustments this week based off that list you gave me."

"Wow, Karie. You didn't have to do that." Genevieve accepted the spine-cracking hug his mother was known for giving. Sunlight glittered off the line of tears in her eyes as Karie pulled away.

"Course I did, honey. You're family. It's my job to make sure you're taken care of. Besides, it makes the ranch a bit more accessible to those in wheelchairs who still want the benefits of the great outdoors." Karie patted Genevieve's hand but refused to let go, and Easton had never felt lighter. His mother pushed at his chest so she could take over driving, leaving him in the dust. "Well, come on now, let's test this sucker out."

Genevieve and his mother climbed the ramp to the front door, but Easton could only marvel at the expanse of wilderness and beauty around him. In the distance, he caught sight of the project he and Weston had been building these past few months. It was hard work constructing something that big from scratch, but their father had taught them right, and he and his brother had worked well together after he'd dug up Weston's childhood bear. He shook his head. The things he did for the woman he loved.

Weston was in the process of recruiting more reserve officers, but they'd managed to make Easton's new part-time schedule work. Three days a week, he was here in Battle Mountain with Genevieve working her cases remotely, and the rest of the time they spent in Alamosa for her court proceedings and in-office administration. Judges, clerks and assistants alike had been all too willing to accommodate her needs. Their new routine was about to change through.

Easton jogged up the cabin's front steps and into the house where he'd always felt welcome. Heat wrapped around him the moment he stepped over the threshold. A massive stone fireplace climbed two stories up the open main living space. Builder-grade wood, lighter than the exterior of the cabin, absorbed the sunlight penetrating through floor-to-ceiling windows on one end of the structure. His grandmother's frayed multicolored crocheted rug took up a majority of the hardwood floor in the front room. A small carved bear holding a bowl of fruit he and Weston had always been too rough with greeted him from the table stretching along the back of the dark leather sofa. Similar carvings had been strategically positioned around the open kitchen and against the grand staircase leading to the bedroom level. Hand-crafted lamps, varying shades of animal fur and muted nature paintings finished the space in old-style hunter decor, and peace tendrilled through him. Every time.

The spice of cooking sausage, and the comforting aroma of biscuits with a hint of heavy cream dove into his lungs. Biscuits and gravy. His favorite. Karie maneuvered Genevieve and her chair to one end of the table as Weston and Chloe took up the other. Small talk filled the room as Easton gripped the back of the head chair. His father's chair. He scanned the smiles and relaxed into the warmth filling the house, memorizing everything he could about this moment. A year ago, he'd isolated himself in one of the satellite cabins, content to live with his demons. Now, after a few months of therapy and taking care of Genevieve's needs, he couldn't imagine living the rest of his life alone.

"Your father would've loved this. Having all of you here for breakfast. Any meal really. The man loved his food, but he loved this family more." His mother pulled out the chair and nodded. "Take a seat, Easton. It's yours now."

A knot of hesitation twisted in his gut, but the rest of the family kept about as though nothing had changed. They exchanged plates, their silverware clinking against glass. They filled their cups with juice and mugs with coffee and caught up with their weeks and went on about their lives. Easton took his seat at the head of the table. Grasping his spoon, he tapped it against the side of his juice glass as his mother sat at the other end. He cleared his throat, nerves shot to hell and back. "I, uh, have an announcement for you all."

Genevieve's smile slipped from her mouth as she eyed him. The realization the ramp out front wasn't why he'd brought her here this morning widened her eyes. She lowered her voice. "What are you doing?"

"Genevieve, these past three months, building a life with you and confronting the demons in my head have changed my life. I never imagined I could ever be this happy, and it's because of you I was finally able to find the purpose my father always wished for me." He set down his juice, his grip too tight. "The past few weekends when I told you I was coming out here to work, Weston and I were building a recovery facility for returning soldiers and trauma survivors. Whispering Pines played a key role in protecting me since my discharge, gave me someplace I felt safe. And with Mom's and the town's permission, now it'll help others like you and me."

Genevieve tossed her napkin onto the table as though she intended to stand. Instead, she leaned over the side of her chair and reached for him. Her fingers slipped along his jaw, and he met her the rest of the way. "Easton, that's amazing. You've been working on the facility this whole time, and you didn't tell me?"

"I wanted it to be a surprise." He pressed his mouth to hers, and a feeling of completeness, of wholeness, filled his chest. "There's still the matter of a few permits, and we're on the hunt for certified psychologists and physical therapists specializing in trauma, but we should have everything up and running within the year. Even have a couple potential patients in line. I know you love your job, and we want to stay in Alamosa, but this way, you'll have somewhere to do your physical therapy without breaking your routine when we come to Battle Mountain."

Clapping and hollers echoed off the walls.

"I'm so proud of you." Genevieve set her forehead against his, her smile destroying the last reservations he'd carried since their wedding day all those years ago.

Another round of clinking glass dragged his attention from the loving depths of her eyes. Weston stood, his juice glass raised, and his arm latched around his fiancée. "Turns out, we've got some good news, too. Chloe and I are pregnant."

As delirious happiness shot through Easton, he started a second round of applause and hoots. Hell, he was going to be an uncle. Who would've thought?

"Oh!" Karie Ford jumped from her seat and raced around the table. Enveloping Weston and Chloe in one of her bone-crushing hugs, his mother nearly started jumping up and down. "I knew it. Congratulations!"

"Congratulations!" both he and Genevieve said. He intertwined his fingers with hers on the surface of the table then brought the back of her hand to his mouth. The past three months had been filled with the unknown, a desperation for normalcy and finding their pace, but Easton didn't have any doubt in his mind he and Genevieve would be making an announcement of their own soon.

The diamond engagement ring he'd worked two jobs to afford fifteen years ago weighed heavy in his pocket. He'd kept it on him since the day he'd found it in the church's bridal room, through his escape into the wilderness and war. Not waiting for the right moment or the right woman. Waiting for her. And when the time was right, Easton would get down on one knee and make them partners. Forever. "Here's to the future, Counselor."

"The future." Genevieve pressed his hand against her check. "Whatever it may hold."

Epilogue

She set a timer. Two minutes.

That was all the time she had to get out of the house.

Alma Majors slid her feet into the shoes she kept under the bed as quietly as possible. Her husband didn't take long to go to the restroom in the middle of the night, but this was her only chance of escape. Her wrist protested as she twisted the doorknob to their shared bedroom open.

One minute.

She was down the stairs and pulling her go bag from the top of the linen closet.

The kitchen lights flicked on. "What are you doing?"

Fear skittered up her spine. She curled her uninjured hand into the thick fabric of the duffel bag. Six years. They were supposed to be happy. They were supposed to be in love, but something had changed. Alma turned to face him. "I couldn't sleep. Figured I'd head to the treadmill downstairs for a quick run to see if that helped."

She slid the hand he'd slammed in the car door into the bag, felt for the solid weight she'd never thought she'd need.

He maneuvered around the kitchen island, setting down the glass of water. He'd tricked her. He'd made it sound as though he'd been using the bathroom and come down here instead. She wasn't sure how. It didn't matter. "You and I both know that's not where you were thinking of going, Alma. Come on. We've talked about this. You have nowhere else to go. No one who will believe you."

"You're right about one of those things." Three hard knocks echoed from the front door, and every nerve ending in her body flinched at the overly loud sound.

"Who is that? Who did you call?" He stepped toward her, his eyes nothing but pools of fire.

She secured her grip around the weapon she'd hid in the bag, pulled it free and took aim. "Don't come any closer. I'm warning you." Alma sidestepped toward the door. If she didn't answer it, the officer on the other side would kick it in. "I'm leaving, and you can't stop me."

Another three knocks from the front door. This time harder.

"It wasn't supposed to be like this." He was supposed to be in the bathroom. Her hands shook as she clung to the unfamiliar weapon. This wasn't her. She didn't handle guns. She extracted artifacts of the rarest kind and showed them to the world. Alma fumbled for the doorknob, the gun heavier than she imagined it would be. The dead bolt. She had to unlock the dead bolt. "Don't come looking for me. I don't ever want to see you again. Understand?"

"You're making the biggest mistake of your life, Alma." The warning was there in his voice, and the muscles down her spine tightened in preparation for what came next.

"No." She swung the front door open. "I'm saving my life."

The man on the other side stepped over the threshold, so much bigger than she remembered in the emergency room that day he'd come looking for the district attorney from Alamosa. Reserve officer Easton Ford stared down her husband as she recalled their conversation, how he'd known exactly what'd happened to her and who had inflicted the damage to her hand. "Ms. Majors, I'm here to escort you from the house. Is that going to be a problem?"

Alma lowered the weapon and handed it over to Officer Ford. She didn't know where she'd go now, what would happen next, but it couldn't be worse than this. She was ready to take back her life, to learn how to protect herself, and she'd start right now. "No. I'm ready."

* * * * *

*Bad things have been happening to Buckhorn residents,
and Darby Fulton's sure it has something to do with
a new store called Gossip. As a newspaper publisher,
she can't ignore the story, any more than she can resist
being drawn to former cop Jasper Cole.
Their investigation pulls them both into a twisted
scheme of revenge where secrets are a deadly weapon…*

*Read on for a sneak preview of
Before Buckhorn,
part of the Buckhorn, Montana series,
by New York Times bestselling author B.J. Daniels.*

Saturday evening the crows came. Jasper Cole looked
up from where he'd been standing in his ranch kitchen
cleaning up his dinner dishes. He'd heard the rustle of
feathers and looked up with a start to see several dozen
crows congregated on the telephone line outside.

Just the sight of them stirred a memory of a time
dozens of crows had come to his grandparents' farmhouse
when he was five. The chill he felt at both the memory
and the arrival of the crows had nothing to do with the
cool Montana spring air coming in through the kitchen
window.

He stared at the birds, noticing that they all seemed
to be watching him. There were so many of them, their
ebony bodies silhouetted against a cloudless sky, their

shiny dark eyes glittering in the growing twilight. As this murder of crows began to caw, he listened as if this time he might decode whatever they'd come to tell him. But like last time, he couldn't make sense of it. Was it another warning, one he was going to wish that he'd heeded?

Laughing to himself, he closed the window and finished his dishes. He didn't really believe the crows were a portent of what was to come this time—any more than last time. His grandmother had, though. He remembered watching her cross herself and mumble a prayer as if the crows were an omen of something sinister on its way. As it turned out, she'd been right.

At almost forty, Jasper could scoff all he wanted, even as a bad feeling settled deep in his belly. That feeling only worsened as the crows suddenly all took flight as if their work was done.

Over the next few days, he would remember the evening the crows appeared. It was the same day Leviathan Nash arrived in Buckhorn, Montana, to open his shop in the old carriage house and strange things had begun to happen—even before people started dying.

Don't miss
Before Buckhorn *by B.J. Daniels,*
available February 2022 wherever
HQN books and ebooks are sold.

HQNBooks.com